Danielle Evans is an Associate Profess[...]
and the author of two short story coll[...]
Corrections and *Before You Suffocate* [...]
collection won the PEN America PEN/Robert W. Bingham Prize,
the Hurston/Wright Legacy Award for fiction, and the Paterson
Prize for fiction; her second won the Janet Heidinger Kafka Prize
and The Bridge Book Award and was a finalist for the Aspen Words
Literary Prize, The Story Prize, and the *Los Angeles Times* Book
Prize for Fiction. She is the 2021 winner of the New Literary Project
Joyce Carol Oates Prize, a 2020 National Endowment for the Arts
fellow, and a 2011 National Book Foundation 5 under 35 honoree.

'Danielle Evans's whipsmart first story collection charts the liminal
years between childhood and the condition dubiously known as
being a grown-up . . . Fiercely independent, all of Evans's characters struggle for a place in a world intent of fencing them out. But
as her title suggests, the biggest obstacles they face are often their
own selves.'   *The New York Times Book Review*

'Danielle Evans's blisteringly smart short stories offer fresh perspec-
tive on being young and black in America. From a vandalizing
valedictorian to a rejected biracial child, her characters triumph by
surviving without forgetting.'   *Time*

'The most vivid characters in Danielle Evans's story collection are
in-betweeners: between girlhood and womanhood; between the
black middle class and Ivy League privilege; between iffy boyfriends
and those even less reliable; between an extended family and living
on your own. To say they're caught between worlds isn't quite
accurate, though; they tend to be hard-headed, sadder but wiser
and, most of all, funny.'   *The New York Times*

Also by Danielle Evans

The Office of Historical Corrections

Before You Suffocate Your Own Fool Self

Danielle Evans

PICADOR

First published 2010 by Riverhead Books
an imprint of Penguin Random House LLC

First published in the UK 2023 by Picador
an imprint of Pan Macmillan
The Smithson, 6 Briset Street, London EC1M 5NR
EU representative: Macmillan Publishers Ireland Ltd, 1st Floor,
The Liffey Trust Centre, 117–126 Sheriff Street Upper,
Dublin 1, D01 YC43
Associated companies throughout the world
www.panmacmillan.com

ISBN 978-1-5290-7323-2

Copyright © Danielle Evans 2010

The right of Danielle Evans to be identified as the
author of this work has been asserted by her in accordance
with the Copyright, Designs and Patents Act 1988.

The following stories have been published previously, in slightly different form: "Virgins" (*The Paris
Review*), "Harvest" (*Phoebe*), "Someone Ought to Tell Her There's Nowhere to Go" (*A Public Space*),
"The King of a Vast Empire" (*5 Chapters*), and "Robert E. Lee Is Dead" (*Black Renaissance Noire*).

"The Bridge Poem" by Donna Kate Rushin used by permission of the author.

"Between Ourselves" Copyright © 1976 by Audre Lorde, from *The Collected Poems of Audre Lorde* by
Audre Lorde. Used by permission of W. W. Norton & Company, Inc.

9 8 7 6 5 4 3 2 1

A CIP catalogue record for this book is available from the British Library.

Printed and bound by CPI Group (UK) Ltd, Croydon, CR0 4YY

MIX
Paper | Supporting
responsible forestry
FSC® C116313

Visit www.picador.com to read more about all our books
and to buy them. You will also find features, author interviews and
news of any author events, and you can sign up for e-newsletters
so that you're always first to hear about our new releases.

I'm sick of mediating with your worst self
On behalf of your better selves

I am sick
Of having to remind you
To breathe
Before you suffocate
Your own fool self

—DONNA KATE RUSHIN, "The Bridge Poem"

I do not believe our wants
have made all our lies holy.

—AUDRE LORDE, "Between Ourselves"

Contents

Virgins

Me and Jasmine and Michael were hanging out at Mr. Thompson's pool. We were fifteen and it was the first weekend after school started, and me and Jasmine were sitting side by side on one of Mr. Thompson's ripped-up green-and-white lawn chairs, doing each other's nails while the radio played "Me Against the World." It was the day after Tupac got shot, and even Hot 97, which hadn't played any West Coast for months, wasn't playing anything else. Jasmine kept complaining that Michael smelled like bananas.

"Sunscreen," Jasmine said, "is some white-people shit. That's them white girls you've been hanging out with, got you wearing sunscreen. Black people don't burn."

Never mind that Michael was lighter than Jasmine and I was lighter than Michael, and really all three of us burned. Earlier, when Jasmine had gone to the bathroom, I'd let Michael rub sunscreen gently into my back. I guess I smelled like bananas, too, but I couldn't smell anything but the polish, and I didn't think she could, either. Jasmine was on about some other stuff.

"You smell like food," Jasmine said. "I don't know why you wanna smell like food. Ain't nobody here gonna lick you because you smell like bananas. Maybe that shit works in Bronxville, but not with us."

"I don't want you to lick me," Michael said. "I don't know where your mouth has been. I know you don't never shut it."

"Shut up," I said. They were my only two real friends and if they fought I'd've had to fix it. I turned up the dial on Mr. Thompson's radio, which was big and old. The metal had deep scratches on it, and rust spots left by people like us, who didn't watch to see whether or not we'd flicked drops of water on it. It had a good sound, though. When the song was over they cut to some politician from the city saying again that it was a shame talented young black people kept dying like this, and it was time to do something about it. They'd been saying that all day. Mr. Thompson got up and cut off the radio.

"You live like a thug, you die like a thug," he said, looking at us. "It's nothing to cry over when people wake up in the beds they made."

He was looking for an argument, but I didn't say nothing, and Jasmine didn't, either. Part of swimming in Mr. Thompson's pool was that he was always saying stuff like that. It still beat swimming at the city pool, which had closed for the season last weekend, and before that had been closed for a week after someone got beat up there. When it was open it was crowded and dirty from little kids who peed in it, and was usually full of people who were always trying to start something. People like Michael, who had nothing better to do.

"I'm not crying for nobody," Michael told Mr. Thompson. "Tupac been dead to me since he dissed B.I.G." He looked up and made some bootleg version of the sign of the cross, like he was talking about God or something. He must've seen it in a movie.

Mr. Thompson shook his head at us and walked back to the lawn chair where he'd been reading the paper. He let it crinkle loudly when he opened it again, like even the sound of someone else reading would make us less ignorant.

Jasmine snorted. She lifted Michael's sweatshirt with the tips of her thumb and index finger so she didn't scratch her still-drying polish and pulled out the pictures he had been showing us before Mr. Thompson came over—photos of his latest girlfriend, a brunette with big eyes and enormous breasts, lying on a bed with a lot of ruffles on it.

"You live like a white girl, you act like a white girl," said Jasmine, frowning at the picture and making her voice deep like she was Mr. Thompson.

"She's not white," said Michael. "She's Italian."

Jasmine squinted at the girl's penny-sized pink nipples. "She look white to me."

"She's Italian," said Michael.

"Italian people ain't white?"

"No."

"What the fuck are they, then?"

"Italian."

"Mr. Thompson," Jasmine called across the yard, "are Italian people white?"

"Ask the Ethiopians," said Mr. Thompson, and none of us knew what the hell he was talking about, so we all shut up for a minute.

The air started to feel cooler through our swimsuits, and Michael got up, putting his jeans on over his wet swim trunks and pulling his sweatshirt over his head. I followed Jasmine into the house, where we took turns changing in the downstairs bathroom. It was an old house, like most of the ones in his part of town, but Mr. Thompson kept it nice: the wallpaper was peeling a little, but the bathroom was clean. The soap in the soap dish was shaped like a seashell, and it seemed like we were the only ones who ever used it. On our way out we said good-bye to Mr. Thompson, who nodded at us and grunted, "Girls"; then, harsher, at Michael: "Boy."

Michael rolled his eyes. Michael wasn't bad. Mostly I thought he hung out with us because he was bored a lot. He needed somebody to chill with when the white girls he was fucking's parents were home. We didn't get him in trouble as much as his boys did. We hung out with him because we figured it was easier to have a boy around than not to. Strangers usually thought one of us was with him, and they didn't know which, so they didn't bother either of us. When you were alone, men were always wanting something from you. We even wondered about Mr. Thompson sometimes, or at least we never went swimming at his house without Michael with us.

Mr. Thompson was retired, but he used to be our elementary school principal, which is how he was the only person in Mount Vernon we knew with a swimming pool in his backyard. We—and everybody else we knew—lived on the south side, where it was mostly apartment buildings, and if you had a house, you were lucky if your backyard was big enough for a plastic kiddie pool. The bus didn't go by Mr. Thompson's house, and it was a twenty-minute walk from our houses even if we walked fast, but it was nicer than swimming at the city pool. We were the only ones he'd told could use his pool anytime.

"It's 'cause I collected more than anyone else for the fourth-grade can drive, when we got the computers," I said. "He likes me."

"Nah," Jasmine said, "he don't even remember that. It's 'cause my mom worked at the school all those years."

Jasmine's mom had been one of the lunch ladies, and we'd gone out of our way to pretend not to know her, with her hairnet cutting a line into her broad forehead, her face all covered in sweat. Even when she got home she'd smell like grease for hours. Sometimes if my mother made me a bag lunch, I'd split it with Jasmine so we didn't have to go through the lunch line and hear the other kids laugh. At school, Mr. Thompson had been nicer to Jasmine's mother than we had. We felt bad for letting Mr. Thompson make us nervous. He was the smartest man either of us knew, and probably he was just being nice. We were not stupid, though. We'd had enough nice guys suddenly look at us the wrong way.

My first kiss was with a boy who'd said he'd walk me home and a block later was licking my mouth. The first time a guy had ever touched me—like touched me *there*—I was eleven and he was sixteen and a lifeguard at the city pool. We'd been playing chicken and when he put me down he held me against the cement and put his fingers in me, and I wasn't scared or anything, just cold and surprised.

When I told Jasmine later she said he did that to everyone, her too. Michael kept people like that out of our way. People had used to say that he was fucking one of us, or trying to, but it wasn't like that. He was our friend, and he'd moved on to white girls from Bronxville anyway. It was like he didn't even see us like girls sometimes, and that felt nice because mostly everybody else did.

Michael's brother Ron was leaned up against his car, waiting for him at the bottom of Mr. Thompson's hill. The car was a brown Cadillac that was older than Ron, who graduated from our high school last spring and worked at Radio Shack. People didn't usually notice the car much because they were too busy looking at Ron and he knew it. He was golden-colored, with curly hair and doll-baby eyelashes and the kind of smile where you could count all of his teeth. Jasmine always said how fine he was, but to me he looked like the kind of person who should be on television, not someone you'd actually wanna talk to. He must've still been mad at Pac, too, or he was just tired of hearing him on the radio, because he was bumping Nas from the tape deck. Michael hopped in the front seat and started to wave bye to us.

"Man," Ron said, cuffing him on the back of his head. "You got two cute girls here, and you ain't even gonna try to take 'em with you? I thought I raised you better than that."

"I'm meeting people at the Galleria. You coming?" Michael called.

"Who's gonna be there?" Jasmine asked.

"Me, Darius, Eddie . . . prolly some other people."

"Nuh-uh," Jasmine said. "You're cool, but your boy ain't."

"What's wrong with my boy?" Michael asked, grinning.

Jasmine made a *tsk* sound. "He ignorant, that's what."

"Damn son," said Ron as he walked back to the driver's side. "Your whole crew can't get no play." He got in, slammed the car door, and did a U-turn. On his way past us he leaned out the window and called, "You get tired of messing with these fools, you come down to the mall and see *me*," then rolled up the amber window and drove off.

Jasmine's problem was that she had lost her virginity to Michael's friend Eddie four months before. He told her he would go with her afterward but instead he went with Cindy Jackson. We saw them all over the city all summer, holding hands. It drove Jasmine crazy. Jasmine liked to pretend no one knew any of this, even though JASMINE FUCKED EDDIE AND NOW SHE'S PRESSED!! had been written in both the boys' and girls' bathrooms at school for months. Cindy wrote it in both places. I told Jasmine Cindy was probably real familiar with the boys' bathroom.

"The only difference between that girl and the subway," I said, "is that everybody in the world hasn't ridden the subway."

I thought Jasmine would feel better, but instead of laughing she sniffled and said, "He left me for some trashy bitch." After that I just let her cry.

On our way to Jasmine's house, she said, "I'm sad about Tupac, a little. It is sad. You can't ever do anything. I bet you if I got famous, somebody would kill me too."

"What the hell would you get famous for?" I asked.

"I'm just saying, if I did."

"Sure," I said. "You'd be just like Tupac."

"I'm just saying, Erica, you never know. You don't know what could happen. You don't know how much time you got."

Jasmine could be melodramatic like that, thinking because something bad happened somewhere, something bad would happen to you. I remembered when Tupac had went to jail, and Jasmine cried because she said we could get arrested too, and I said, *"For what?"*, but it didn't matter, she just kept crying. Mostly to make her feel better, we had bought IT'S A SET UP SO KEEP YA HEAD UP T-shirts at the mall. My mother screamed when she saw us wearing them.

"Setup," she said. "Y'all take that crap off. Keep believing everything these rap stars tell you. I'm telling you, the minute a man says someone set him up for anything, you run, because he's about to set you up for something."

There were a whole lot of men we were supposed to stay away from according to my mother: rap stars, NBA players, white men. We didn't really know any of those kinds of people. We only knew boys like Michael who freestyled a little but mostly not well, who played ball violently like someone's life was at stake, or else too pretty, flexing for the girls every time they made a decent shot, because even they knew they would never make the NBA, and we were all they were gonna get out of a good game. The only white men we knew were teachers and cops, and no one had to tell us to try and stay away from them, when that was all we did in the first place, but my mother was always worried about something she didn't need to be.

When we got to Jasmine's apartment, we went straight to her room, which felt almost like it was my room too. We lived two blocks from each other and slept at each other's house as much as we slept at our own. My schoolbooks were still piled on the corner of her floor, my second bathing suit was hanging over her desk chair, where I'd left it to dry last weekend. Me and Jasmine always shared everything, and after I showered I went through Jasmine's closet like I would have gone through mine, looking for something to wear out later. Only this year was sharing things getting to be a problem, because we were starting to be built different. I put on a pair of Jasmine's jeans, which were tight around my hips and she told me so. "Look at you, stretching out my jeans with your big old ass," was what she actually said.

"You wish you had my ass," I said, which was true, she did, because hers was flat like a board and people teased her about it. Jasmine was small but all the meat she had on her was settled in her tummy, which was a cute little puff now but would be a gut someday if she ever got fat. It made me happy sometimes to think that even though Jasmine's face was better than mine, if I ever got fat I'd get fat the way my mother had, all in the hips and chest, and some people would still be all right with that, more than if I had a big giant stomach like Jasmine might one day. We weren't bad-looking, neither one of us, but we weren't ever going to be beautiful, either, I knew that already. We were the kind of girls who would always be very pretty *if* but *if* never seemed to happen. If Jasmine's skin cleared up and she could keep her hair done and she did something about her teeth, which were a little crooked, and if I lost five pounds and got contact lenses and did something about the way my skin was always ashy, maybe we'd be the prettiest girls in Mount Vernon, but we weren't, we were just us. Jasmine had beautiful dark eyes and the most perfect nose I ever saw on anybody, and I had nice lips and a pretty good shape, and that was it. We got dressed to go to the movies because there was nothing else to do, and even though Jasmine's pants were a little tight on me and the shirt I'd borrowed was pushing my chest up in my face, I looked all right, just maybe like I was trying too hard.

When we got to the lobby of the new movie theatre, I told Jasmine I liked the way it was done up: the ceiling was gold and glittery and the carpet was still fire-truck red and not dingy burgundy like red carpet usually was. Jasmine said she thought the whole thing looked fake and tacky, and speaking of fake and tacky, look who was here. It was Cindy, in some tight jeans and a shirt that said BABY GIRL and showed off the rhinestone she had stuck to her belly button. Eddie was there, too, and Michael and a bunch of their friends, and they waved us over. When Cindy saw Jasmine she ran up and hugged her, and Jasmine hugged her back, like they hadn't been calling each other skank-ass bitches five minutes ago. The boys all looked confused, because boys are stupid like that.

"Look what Eddie gave me," said Cindy, all friendly. She pulled a pink teddy bear out of her purse and squeezed its belly. It sang *You are my sunshine*, in a vibrating robot voice. It scared me.

"That's nice," said Jasmine, her voice so high that she sounded almost like the teddy bear. Cindy smiled and walked off to go kiss on Eddie some more. She was swinging her hips back and forth like the pendulum our science teacher had showed us, as if anyone was really trying to look at her.

"Instigator," I whispered to Jasmine as Cindy left. Jasmine ignored me.

"I don't have a teddy bear, neither," said Eddie's friend Tre, putting an arm around Jasmine. Jasmine pushed his arm off.

"C'mon, Jasmine. I lost my teddy bear. Can I sleep with you tonight?"

All Eddie's friends had been trying to push up on Jasmine since they found out she'd done it with him, but Jasmine wasn't having it. She looked at Tre like he was some nasty-flavored gum on the bottom of her shoe. She'd told me next time she was waiting for the real thing, not some punk high school boy. Michael put an arm around each of our shoulders and kissed us both on the cheek, me first, then Jasmine.

"You know these are my girls," he said to Tre. "Leave 'em alone."

He didn't need to mention me, but I felt good that he had. His friends mostly left me alone already, because they knew I wasn't good for anything but kissing you a little bit and running away. Michael nodded good-bye as he and his friends walked toward their movie. Eddie and Cindy stayed there, kissing, like that's what they had paid admission for anyway. I grabbed Jasmine's hand and pulled her in the other direction.

"That's nasty," I said. "She looks nasty all up on him in public like that."

"No one ever bought me a singing teddy bear," said Jasmine as we walked to the ticket counter. "Probably no one ever will buy me a singing teddy bear."

"I'll buy you a singing teddy bear, you silly bitch," I said.

"Shut up," she said. She had been sucking on her own bottom lip so hard she'd sucked the lipstick off it, and her lips were two different colors. "Don't you ever want to matter to somebody?"

"I matter to you," I said. "And Michael."

Jasmine clicked her tongue. "Michael," she said. "Say Michael had to shoot either you or that Italian chick who's letting him hit it right now. Who do you think he would save?"

"Why does he have to shoot somebody?" I said.

"He just does."

"Well, he'd save me, then. She's just a girl who's fucking him."

"And you're just a girl who isn't," Jasmine said. "You don't understand anything, do you? Look . . ." She whirled me around and pointed at Cindy Jackson, who had her arms wrapped around Eddie and his hand scrunched in her hair. "When are we going to be that kind of girl?"

"What, the stupid kind? Everyone knows he's messing with that girl who works at the earring place at the Galleria. Probably other girls too."

"That's not even the point, stupid. She's the one he kisses in public."

"Well, that's her own dumb fault, I don't see why you gotta be worried about it," I said. "I wouldn't kiss that idiot in public if you paid me. I wouldn't kiss his fingernail in public."

Jasmine kept watching them kiss for a minute, and she looked real sad, like she might cry or something. "That's your problem, Erica, you don't understand adult relationships," she said.

"Where are there adults?" I asked, looking around. I put my hand to my forehead like I was a sea captain looking for dry land, and turned around in circles, but everywhere it was the same old people doing the same old things.

"You're right," Jasmine said. "I'm tired of these little boys. Next weekend we're going to the city. We're gonna find some real niggas who know how to treat us."

That was not the idea I meant for Jasmine to have.

We had our cousins' IDs, and we'd been clubbing a few times before, in Mount Vernon, but it wasn't the same. It was usually just a bar with a DJ, and someone always knew us; we never stayed that long or got into any real trouble. Once we were inside, people would appear out of nowhere, all *Ain't you Miss Trellis's daughter?* or *Didn't you used to be friends with my little sister?* If we flirted even a little bit, someone would show up to say, *Yo, those are some little girls right there,* and our guy would vanish. Sometimes a guy would get mad and report us to the bouncer, who would tell us it was time to go home. *You had your fun, girls,* he'd say, and the thing was, usually we had. The point was getting in and saying we'd been there. Clubbing in the city was something else.

In a TV sitcom, one of our mothers would have called the other and busted us, but Jasmine's mom worked nights at a diner in Yonkers, and my mom passed out around ten, two hours after she got home from working as a secretary in White Plains, and no one was making any TV show about the two of us so that was that. Her mom thought I was at her house and my mom thought she was at my house, and meanwhile we were standing on the platform of the MTA toward Manhattan.

Jasmine wouldn't let me wear panty hose, because I'd borrowed her shoes that opened at the toe and laced up my leg from my ankles to just below my knee, and I felt naked: Her skirt was too short on me. The only thing Jasmine let me do right was bring Michael with us, and he was standing there in his brother's shoes, since he only owned Tims and sneakers. He also had his brother's ID, even though his brother didn't look a damn thing like him. Michael was smaller and copper-colored and looked to me like he ought to wear glasses, even though he didn't.

"Money earnin' Mount Vernon's not good enough for you two anymore?" he asked, his hands stuffed in his jeans' pockets.

"Mount Vernon's not good enough for anybody," said Jasmine.

"And this city needs a new damn motto. Do you know anybody here who earns any real money?"

"Mr. Thompson's doing all right," Michael said, and I thought to turn around and see if Mr. Thompson was standing on the platform watching me, because I knew if he was he'd be disappointed.

It hadn't finished turning into night yet when we'd gotten on the train, but when we got off in the city my legs shivered. It was still early, so we got slices of pizza from Famous Ray's, and sat in the window, watching people go by. Our reflections in the window glass looked watery, like we were melting at the edges.

"All right," said Jasmine. "Who are we tonight?"

"Serene and Alexis, same as always," I said, "And Michael, you're Ron, I guess." I was thinking of the names on our IDs.

"No, stupid. I mean, who are we when guys ask questions?" Jasmine said.

"Seniors?" I said.

"Nah, we're in college," said Jasmine.

"What college?" I said.

"You two? Clown College," said Michael. Jasmine threw a dirty napkin at him.

"That's you, Michael," she said. "We in City College. I'm a fashion major, and I'ma get rich selling people nice clothes so girls don't go around lookin' like Cindy Jackson, lookin' trifling all the time, and so you, Erica, can find some pants that actually fit your ass in them. I got a man, and he's fine, and he plays ball, but I may have to kick him to the curb because lately he's jealous of me, so I'm at the club lookin' for someone who can handle me."

"What's he jealous for?" I asked.

"He's jealous of my success, dummy. Who are you?"

I thought about what I would be if I could be anything, but I didn't really know.

"I'm at City College, too, I guess," I said. "What do you major in to be a teacher?"

"Teaching," said Jasmine.

"Ain't no major in teaching," said Michael.

"You ever been to college?" said Jasmine "Your brother ain't even been to college."

"I'm not stupid," said Michael. "I'm gonna have a degree. I was over at Mr. Thompson's today talking about books and stuff, while you two were putting a bunch of makeup on your faces."

"Whatever," I said. "Teaching. I'm majoring in teaching, then."

"What about your man?" Jasmine said.

"He's great," I said. "He's in college, too, and he's gonna be a doctor, but he also writes me love poems. And paints pictures of me. He's a painter too."

"He so great, why you at the club?" said Michael.

"Umm . . . he's dead?" I said.

"Dead?" said Jasmine.

"Dead." I nodded. "I just finished grieving. I burned all his poems and now I wish I still had them."

"Check this chick," said Jasmine. "Even when she makes shit up, her life is fucked up."

. . .

Michael gave me his jacket on the way from Ray's to the club, and I wrapped it around me and felt warmer. He was talking about earlier, when he was over at Mr. Thompson's.

"Did you know," said Michael, "that the Ethiopians beat the Italian army?"

"Do I care?" Jasmine asked. "No wonder I never meet nobody, hanging out with you."

Michael made a face at Jasmine behind her back, but we were quiet for the rest of the walk.

I didn't know why Jasmine needed to meet people besides us anyway. Jasmine thought just because people were older, they were going to be more interesting. They didn't look any more interesting, all lined up outside the club like we did on school picture day. At the door one of the bouncers checked Jasmine's ID, then looked her up and down and waved her in. He barely looked at mine, just glanced at my chest and stamped my hand. But he didn't even take Michael's, just shook his head at him and laughed.

"Not tonight," he said.

Michael didn't look too surprised, but he reached for my wrist when he saw I was waiting there, like I would have left with him if he asked me.

"You be careful with yourself, all right?"

I nodded. The bouncer turned around like he might change his mind about letting me in. "Bye, Ron," said Jasmine, and she took off.

I ran in after her. "You didn't have to just leave him like that."

She rolled her eyes. "Whole room full of people and you're worried about Michael. He can take care of himself."

I knew Michael would be all right. It was me I was worried about. The dance floor was full, and the strobe light brought people in and out of focus like holograms. Up on the metal platforms girls were dancing in shorts and bikini tops. The one closest to me had her body bent in half, her hands on her ankles and her shiny-gold-short-covered butt in the air. I wondered how you got to be a girl like that. Did you care too much what other people thought, or did you stop caring?

Me and Jasmine did what we always did at a club, moved to the center of the dance floor and moved our hips to the music. By the end of the first song two men had come up behind us and started grinding. I looked up at Jasmine to make sure it wasn't Godzilla behind me, and when she nodded and gave me a thumbs-up, I pressed into the guy harder, winding forward and backward. At school they got mad about dancing like that, but we never learned any other kind of dancing except the steps from music videos, and good luck finding a boy who could keep up with that.

After we'd been dancing for an hour and I was sweaty and my thighs were tired, we went to the bathroom to fix ourselves. Nothing could be done about your hair once it started to sweat out, and I was glad at least I had pinned most of it up so you couldn't see the frizzy parts too well. I let Jasmine fix my makeup. I could feel her fingers on my face, fixing my eye shadow, smoothing on my lip gloss. I remembered a book we'd read in middle school and said, "It's like I'm Helen Keller, and you're Teacher."

"You're the teacher," Jasmine said. "I'm Alexis, the fashion designer."

"We're not," I said, because it seemed important all of a sudden, but Jasmine was already on her way out the door.

When we left the bathroom we stood by the bar awhile and waited for people to buy us drinks. I used to always drink Midori sours because they tasted just like Kool-Aid, but Jasmine told me I couldn't keep drinking those because that was the easiest way to show you were underage. I tried different drinks on different guys. A lawyer from Brooklyn bought me something too strong when I told him to surprise me, and kept talking about the river view from his apartment while I tried to drink it in little tiny sips. A construction worker from Queens told me he'd been waiting all his life for me, which must've been a pretty long time because he was kind of old. A real college student, from Harlem, walked away from me when he kept asking me questions about City College and I couldn't answer them right. *Go home, sweetie,* he said, but I couldn't, so I tried other names and stories. I was Renee and Yolanda and Shameka. I was a record store clerk and a waitress and a newspaper photographer. It was easy to be somebody else when no one cared who you were in the first place.

I realized after a while that I didn't see Jasmine anymore. I listened for her, but all I could hear was other people talking, and the boom of music from the speakers above me. Then I heard her laugh on the other side of the bar and start to sing along with Foxy Brown, *Ain't no nigga like the one I got.* She was sitting on a silver bar chair, and there were guys all around her. One of them was telling her how pretty she sang, which was a lie: she had no voice to begin with, plus she was making it sound all stupid and breathy on purpose. When she saw me looking at her, she waved.

"Yo," she said, smiling big like she had the only other time I'd seen her drunk. "Serene." I'd forgotten which name I was answering to and looked at her funny for a minute. I walked closer and one of the men put his arm around me.

"She can come too," he said, and Jasmine smiled, and when she got up for real, I wondered where everyone was going.

I followed Jasmine until I realized we were leaving the club. It was like my whole body blinked. The club had been hot and sticky and outside it was almost cold. The floodlights on the block were so bright that for a minute I thought the sun must have never gone down all the way; it was that light outside.

"The hell?" I said.

"We're going to an after party," she giggled. "In the Bronx. The valet is getting their car. I was just about to look for you."

"No." I shook my head.

"Yes," she said, putting her arms around me and kissing me on the forehead. One of the guys whistled.

The valet pulled the car up, and I counted the men for the first time. There were four of them and two of us and one Mazda 626.

"There's no room," I said. "Let's go." I started to pull Jasmine's hand, but the man by the far window patted his lap, and Jasmine crawled into the car and sat there and put her arms around him.

"Room now," Jasmine said, and because I was out of excuses I got in the car, and five minutes later we were speeding up the West Side Highway. I remembered a story that had been on the news a few weeks ago. Some girl upstate had ended up in the hospital after she went home with five men she met on the bus. They didn't say on the news exactly what they'd done to her, only that she was lucky to be alive. "What was that child thinking, going anyplace with all those strangers?" my mother had said. I wanted to call my mother right then and say she wasn't, Mama, she wasn't thinking at all, one minute she was one place and the next she was another and it all happened before she could stop it.

Then I thought maybe I was overreacting. Lots of people went to other people's houses and most of them didn't end up dead. Jasmine's new friends didn't really look dangerous. They looked like they'd spent more time getting dressed than me and Jasmine had. The one Jasmine was sitting on had a sparkly diamond earring. The one next to me had on a beige linen shirt. They all smelled like cologne beneath sweat. I liked that smell. My sheets had smelled like that once after Michael took a nap in my bed, and I didn't want to wash them until it went away. I felt better. If I was going to kill somebody, I thought, I would not get all dressed up first. I would not put on a lot of perfume. When I turned away from the window to look at the people in the car again, I saw that Jasmine was kissing the man with the earring. She was kissing him deep, and I could see half her tongue going in and out of his mouth. His hands were tracing the top of her shirt. He fingered the chain she always wore around her neck, and stopped kissing her to look at it.

"Princess," he mumbled. "Are you a princess?"

Jasmine giggled. Her chain glittered like a dime at the bottom of a swimming pool.

"Are you a princess too?" the man next to me asked. He looked down at me, and I could see that his eyes were a pretty green, but bloodshot.

"No," I said. I folded my arms across my chest.

"Man, look who we got here," said the one in the passenger seat, turning around. "College girl with a attitude problem. How'd we end up with these girls again? Y'all are probably virgins, aren't you?"

"No," Jasmine said. "Like hell we are. We look like virgins to you?"

"Nah," he said, and I didn't know whether to feel pissed off or pretty.

The car stopped in front of an apartment building, and I followed them into the lobby and into the elevator, and earring guy still had his arms around Jasmine and pretty-eyes guy was still looking at me. If I'd wanted to lose my virginity to a random guy in the Bronx, I would've done it already, not just let Jasmine give it away. I knew if she saw my face, she would know how mad I was, but she had her head in earring guy's neck. The clicks and dings in the elevator seemed like they were saying something in a language I didn't speak. I thought about pulling her off of him. I thought about hitting her. They'd pushed the button for the eighth floor, but the doors opened on five. There was nobody standing there and I kept waiting for the thing that would stop us, and then I thought, Nothing will stop this but me. So I ran, out of the elevator and down the stairs and out the front door and down to the bodega on the corner.

There was a whole pile of fruit lit up outside, like what anybody really needed in the middle of the night was a mango. Inside, it was comforting just looking at the rows and rows of bread and cereal and soup all crammed together, and I stared at them for a while. There was an old man behind the counter, and I thought it was too late for him to be working, and he was looking at me like he thought it was too late for me to be alone in his store. He looked like how I would have imagined my grandfather looking if I'd known him.

"You all right?" he said. "You need some medicine? Some ginger ale?"

I shook my head, because I was looking for Jasmine to be behind me, but she wasn't.

"You need to call somebody?"

I pointed at the pay phone outside on the corner, and the man behind the counter shrugged. When I realized Jasmine wasn't running after me, I walked back outside. The door jingled at me when I opened it, and I was mad at it for sounding so happy. I didn't know who else to call at two-thirty in the morning, so I beeped Michael and pushed in the pay phone number. I was afraid at first he wouldn't call back, but he did, ten minutes later.

"Just come get me," I said, instead of explaining, and all he asked for was the street names.

I'd been leaning against the pay phone for twenty minutes when his brother's car pulled up. Michael was in the passenger's seat. He got out when he saw me, and gave me a hug.

"You all right?" he asked. "Did something happen?" I nodded, then shook my head. I was starting to feel stupid, because I knew I looked a mess, and nothing really had happened to me.

"Where's your girl?"

"Up in one of those buildings, with some guys she met at the club."

Michael's face wrinkled like it was made of clay and I had squished it. "Do we need to go get her?"

I thought of Jasmine in that man's lap, Jasmine laughing and saying *Like hell we are,* Jasmine letting me run out of the elevator by myself.

"No. Leave that trick where she is," I said. Once I said the words I was sorry, but it seemed like the kind of thing you couldn't take back. I wanted Michael to be mad at me, to say he was Jasmine's friend, too, and he wouldn't leave her like that, but he just shrugged at his brother and opened the car door.

"Uh-uh," said Ron, when Michael started to get in the front seat. "Let the lady up front."

I sat beside him while Michael scowled and got in the back.

"I guess we can't take you home to your mom's or you'll be in trouble, huh?" Ron asked.

I wanted to say yes, they could take me home, that I deserved to be in trouble, that I'd let my mother slap me if it meant we'd go get Jasmine and both of us could be at home sleeping in our rooms tonight, but I didn't.

"No," I said. "Can I stay at your place? I'm s'posed to be at Jasmine's."

"No doubt," he said, and squeezed my knee, stopping to look at me so hard that I wasn't even sure what I'd said, but I wanted to take that back too. I remembered my mother saying no one does you a favor who doesn't want something back sometime. Ron was driving already and I looked out the window again and listened to the radio. Even this time of night they were still playing Tupac, which they never would have been doing when he was still alive.

Inside at Michael and Ron's house, they put me on the downstairs couch and gave me a blanket. When Ron said good night and went into his bedroom in the basement, I thought maybe I'd only imagined the look he gave me earlier. I unlaced my shoes and took down my hair and curled up in the blanket, trying not to think about Jasmine and what kind of a mess I'd left her in. I thought of her laughing, thought of the look on her face when she had closed her eyes and let that man kiss her, and for a second I hated her and then a second later I couldn't remember anything I'd ever hated more than leaving her. I was sitting there in the dark when Ron came back and put an arm around me.

"You know, you're too pretty for me to leave you on the couch like that," he said, pulling me toward him. I didn't know that, but I did understand then that there was no such thing as safe, only safer; that this, if it didn't happen now, would happen later but not better. I was safer than Jasmine right now, safer than I might have been. He kissed me, hard, like he was trying to get to the last drop of something, and I kissed him back, harder, like I wanted to get it all back.

The noise in my head stopped and I didn't have to think about anything but where to put all the pieces of my body next.

He grabbed my hand and led me to the bedroom, and he kissed me again and pushed my skirt around my hips. "You're beautiful," he said, which must've been a lie by this time of night. I sat on the bed and pulled my underwear off and realized they were Jasmine's. I thought how mad she'd be that it was me and not her doing this. I kissed him and he kept going and I didn't stop him.

Afterward I was embarrassed because he was embarrassed, and I knew I couldn't stay there, but instead of going back to the couch I walked upstairs to Michael's room and climbed into his bed. He smelled the way I remembered him. I just wanted to touch him, really, and not to wake up alone. But he thought I meant something by it, and I let him. I let him kiss me until he felt under my shirt and his fingers found my bra hook, which was still undone because I hadn't bothered to fasten it.

"What happened?" he asked.

"Nothing," I said.

"Right," he said. He turned away from me and faced the wall. I looked at the back of his ears and thought about a few hours earlier, about him holding my wrist, telling me to be careful with myself. I reached to pull him toward me. I remembered the feeling of his thumb and index finger right there on my pulse as I had nodded yes.

Snakes

The summer I turned nine I went to Tallahassee to visit my grandmother for the first and last time. It was a hot, muggy summer, the kind of weather where you think it's going to storm any minute, but it rarely does. That much hasn't changed in sixteen years—not the weather, not my sense of Tallahassee, then and now, as a place where your skin crawls with the sensation that something urgent is about to happen, but you never know what, or when. That first summer I flew to visit, I was skittish as soon as I exited the plane from New Jersey, escorted by a tight-skirted stewardess who handed me a gold plastic set of pin-on wings before we walked to the arrivals gate.

My grandmother had me picked up from the airport by a driver in a company car. The driver worked for a plastics company that still had my grandfather's name, though he'd been dead since before

I was born. The driver reminded me a little bit of my father—he had the same reddish-brown skin, the same big smile—and while we waited for my luggage to come around the baggage carousel, he gave me a stick of cinnamon bubble gum that I folded and tucked into the pocket of my shorts along with the wings, which I could feel pressing into my leg. My parents, as consolation for shipping me off to my grandmother while they spent the summer in Brazil researching indigenous environmental activism, had loaded my suitcase with books. It was something they did every time they went somewhere without me. Along with the small paperback dictionary my parents had given me last summer, I kept a couple of the new books with me to thumb through on the plane: *Introduction to Rites and Rituals; Talismans: A Photographic Record, Natural Wonders of the Amazon Rain Forest.*

The book on talismans I found particularly intriguing. I looked at pictures of stones and amulets, brightly dyed pieces of fabric, small and elaborately carved sculptures, and wished that I had brought something magical with me. I wondered if gum or plastic was strong enough to be a talisman; I thought of fashioning the wings into a protective necklace. My own interactions with my grandmother had been limited: my mother avoided family events whenever possible, and at the handful I'd accompanied her to, my grandmother had barely spoken to me. She was the only thing in the world I'd ever seen my mother scared of, my mother who told offhand stories about living through monsoons in Asia and military coups in Africa and near encounters with poisonous foot-long centipedes in South America the way other people's mothers talked about what they'd had for dinner the night before. Every time she got off the phone with my grandmother, my mother drank a glass of wine, followed by three cups of Zen tea. My father, who almost never yelled, raised his voice at her from behind their closed bedroom door when she made plans that involved seeing her mother, telling her she ought to know better by now and refusing to go with her. They'd fought over sending me to my grandmother's in the first place, an argument I'd strained my ears to hear and silently hoped my father would win.

Usually when my parents traveled, I stayed with my aunt Claire, my father's sister, but she'd been in poor health, and my mother worried that having me for the summer would be too much for her to keep up with. My father pointed out that I didn't need much keeping up with: I read books, I ate when compelled, I sometimes wrote embellished accounts of my day in a leather-bound black diary. I was the sort of child who generally had to be coerced into playing with other children—the kind whose parents took her to anthropology department cocktail parties so often that their colleagues referred to me as their youngest graduate student—but my mother had said it was too much to impose on Aunt Claire, and anyway, it wasn't me my grandmother hated, it was her, to which my father had responded, *Give her time*. I rolled the words over and over in my head, willing him to be wrong, but if I thought my grandmother would like me better when my mother wasn't around, our reunion quickly disabused me of the thought.

• • •

"Unbelievable," was the first thing my grandmother said when she saw me. From the airport to her house, it had been twenty minutes of loopy, winding roads, packed so densely with trees that looking out the windows from the backseat of the car, I could often see nothing but the green canopies that shaded us. My grandmother's house was at the end of a circular driveway, a white wooden old southern masterpiece, with columns on the front porch and a veranda above it. Coral vines crept gently up its sides, and although it was only four bedrooms inside, at the time I thought of it as a mansion: it could have contained at least three town houses the size of the one I lived in back in Camden. The driver removed my bags from the trunk and walked me up the stairs to the front door. Instinctively, I held his hand as he rang the bell, and squeezed it tighter as the door opened to reveal my grandmother behind it, squinting at me as if her eyes were playing tricks on her.

But for the expression on her face, the way her eyes went from startled to angry as she said *Unbelievable,* she looked remarkably like my mother. They had the same delicate upturned nose and wide brown eyes, and the same fine blond hair, though my mother generally wore hers loose, and my grandmother's was held back in an immaculate twist, and threaded with fine streaks of gray. She stepped out of the doorway and gestured toward the driver with one hand, motioning for him to take my suitcase up the spiral staircase. She ushered me into the house, shutting the door behind me. She gave me a perfunctory kiss on the top of the forehead and reached a hand out to tentatively touch one of my cornrows. She shook her head. "Did your mother do this to you?"

"My hair?" I asked. I looked down at the polished hardwood of the floor beneath me. My mother could barely do my hair herself, and knew I'd never manage to keep it untangled on my own. It was one of those things white mothers of black children learn the hard way once and then tend to remember. Just before I'd left, she had gotten one of her undergraduates to braid my hair in tight pink-lotioned cornrows, so recent they still itched and pulled at my scalp.

"Mommy can't do my hair," I said. "A girl from her school did it for her."

"I swear, even on a different continent, that woman—When you go upstairs, take them out. You're a perfectly decent-looking child, and for whatever reason your mother sends you here looking like a little hoodlum."

"I'm wearing pink," I said, more in my own defense than in my mother's. I had dressed myself, and Aunt Claire had driven me to the airport: my parents had left for Rio the day before. My grandmother considered my argument, evaluated my hot-pink shorts as if prepared to object to them as well, but before she could, my cousin Allison came bounding down the stairs to hug me, blond pigtails flying behind her. When she threw her arms around me and kissed me on the cheek, she smelled strongly of sour-apple Jolly Ranchers and women's perfume that she later confessed she'd stolen from her mother.

"I think you look nice," whispered Allison. She took me upstairs to the room we were sharing for the summer, and then spent the next half-hour helping me undo each braid, my hair spiraling out into tight, disheveled curls. Allison had been my parent's ace in the hole, the only thing that kept me from trying to secretly squeeze myself into one of their suitcases so they'd have to take me to Brazil with them. Her parents were spending the summer on a Caribbean cruise, and my uncle had suggested to my mother that since she'd be at my grandmother's all summer anyway, it might be nice for us to spend some time together. Allison was my playmate at awkward family gatherings, the person I made faces at across the table at Christmas dinner the one year we'd all gathered at her parents' house in Orlando. (It was the last holiday my mother had agreed to spend with her own mother. I'd heard her on the phone last Christmas a year later, saying almost angrily, *No, we're not coming. Last year she said she was dying, and then she didn't.*)

Allison made those first few weeks at my grandmother's house bearable, almost pleasant. I'd never had a backyard before, but at my grandmother's we had an acre of greenery. There was a lawn of impossibly bright grass, landscaped with flowering hydrangea bushes and neatly clipped ornamental shrubbery. Half a mile down the block, the manicured lawns of my grandmother's neighborhood gave way to almost tropical lushness: hanging crape myrtles with vivid pink flowers and twisted, many-stemmed trunks, tall oaks brushed with Spanish moss. When we followed the gravel path off the main road, we found ourselves at a lake about a mile wide; it took us the better part of a day to circle its swampy edges. We shaded ourselves from the thick summer heat by resting underneath one tree after another. The first time we went to the lake, our grandmother admonished us

never to do it again, screamed at us that we had worried her by running off and the lake was a dangerous place for little girls to be alone.
It went in one ear and out the other: we were already in love with
what we'd found there.

It wasn't that my grandmother didn't try. She woke us up one morning with the enthusiastic promise that we'd be going swimming. She
had laid out clothes for us, and though usually when we went to the
pool at home I climbed into the car wearing nothing but my swimsuit and jellies, I wanted my grandmother to be happy with me, and
wore the yellow sundress she'd picked out. Allison's dress was blue,
which matched her eyes, and the bow my grandmother put in her
hair after she brushed it. My grandmother tried to brush my hair,
too, but between the muggy, humid summer air and the ineptitude of
my attempts to control it, it had turned itself into a tangled baby afro,
one that Allison's fine bristled brush did nothing for. That morning
my grandmother set out to comb it into pigtails, but after I began
to cry from the pain of her yanking on my scalp and demanded hair
grease—which of course she didn't have—the comb finally snapped
and my grandmother gave up.

"Maybe the water will help," she said, defeated.

I didn't understand why we needed to be so presentable to go
swimming in the first place—not until she turned into the driveway
of a clubhouse that looked like something out of a fairy tale. Though
we were there to swim, it took us two hours to get anywhere near
the pool. My grandmother walked us around the looping paths of the

private lake, encouraging us to feed the ducks and asserting how pretty the lake was, as if trying to convince us of something. She took us for brunch in the clubhouse; the tables were a dark oak and the ceiling above us was decorated with crisscrossing gold latticework. I made myself dizzy mapping out an imaginary chart of constellations.

Halfway through our pancakes a woman in the tallest heels I'd ever seen a person actually walk in came into the room. "Lydia!" she said when she saw my grandmother. Until then I hadn't thought of my grandmother as having a first name. The woman's skirt swished from side to side when she walked, and up close, the thin brown straps of her high-heeled sandals wrapped delicately around her ankles. She kissed my grandmother on both cheeks and then turned to us expectantly.

"It is so good to see you out again, Lydia," she said. "And who are these little dolls you have with you?"

"Marianne, meet my granddaughters, Allison and Tara," my grandmother said evenly.

Marianne's face flickered for a second, and then resettled into its previous blank enthusiasm.

"Ta-ra," she said, stretching it out like it was two words. "This one must be Amanda's."

Amanda was my mother's name, but the way she said *Amanda*, she might have been saying *the earthquake* or *the flesh-eating disease*. Still, I didn't think much of her identifying me right away. Of course I was my mother's daughter: I had her eyes, her heart-shaped mouth and one-dimpled smile, her round face, only darker.

"Yes, I remember Amanda," Marianne went on. "I guess she never changed, did she?"

"She grew up," said my grandmother, with a nervous laugh.

"They all do," said Marianne, who went on to talk about her sons, an orthodontist and a deputy mayor. My grandmother looked uncomfortable, even after Marianne went to sit at her own table. Though usually she advised us to chew each bite twenty times, because we were young ladies, not wolves, she rushed us through the rest of our breakfast, admonishing us that our eggs were getting cold, even when we could still see the steam rising from them. After the meal, my grandmother relaxed again, but she made us walk around the lake for half an hour in order to let our food digest.

When we finally got to the pool, Allison and I were done with decorum. We threw our sundresses on the hot concrete and cannonballed into the water, ignoring our grandmother's shouts that we should be more careful, and who did we think was going to pick our things up from where we'd left them? We played Marco Polo while our grandmother sunbathed and read the kind of novel I could tell from the cover my mother would have called the waste of a perfectly valuable tree. When we got tired of Marco Polo, we tried doing handstands in the shallow end, and seeing who could hold her breath longest; and when that got boring, we played rock-paper-scissors to see which of us had to get out of the pool and go ask our grandmother for a penny to dive for. I lost. I climbed the ladder and saw that my grandmother had been joined by a woman in sunglasses and a straw hat.

"Grandma," I called, and both women looked up, startled. I asked my grandmother for a penny and she rummaged through her purse to oblige.

"Amanda's, I take it?" the woman beside her asked. She said my mother's name with the same tone as the woman from breakfast. My grandmother nodded.

"What's Amanda up to these days?" the woman asked, pressing her mouth into a thin-lipped smile. She turned away and reached for her sunscreen, as if already bored by the answer.

"She's a doctor," said my grandmother. I opened my mouth to clarify that she wasn't a *doctor* doctor, but my grandmother shooed me away. I started to run off, then slowed down behind her, waiting to hear what else she said about my mother.

"Tara's adopted," my grandmother said. "From Brazil. Amanda's down there now. She always did have a good heart."

Here are some things I didn't know then: The summer she was fifteen, my mother was forever banned from the premises of the Palisade Hills Country Club, after what was later described to me as "a small vandalism incident," in protest of the golf course's de facto segregation policy. The summer she was sixteen, my mother, bristling under my grandmother's restrictions, ran away from home for several months. While she was gone, my grandfather died unexpectedly, and no one knew where to reach her until months after the funeral. My grandmother and my uncles buried him alone, and never let my mother forget it, because no one ever let them. Almost two years before

I came to visit, a small cyst in my grandmother's breast had turned out to be cancerous. My grandmother underwent a mastectomy, radiation, and reconstructive surgery, and was only recently back on her feet. My mother had promised to visit her in the hospital; she didn't.

When we played in her yard, my grandmother usually sat on the porch to watch us, but eventually the phone or some other thing within the house called her away. Allison and I ran. We went for the trees, for the gravel path, for the wonders of the neighborhood or the seclusion of the nearby lake. Away from our grandmother, we mimicked the lives we imagined our parents having in our absence. We'd pretend to be my parents, carrying *Natural Wonders of the Amazon Rain Forest* around the northern Tallahassee suburbs, fancifully misidentifying dozens of plants, insects, and reptiles. We'd harass gardeners and mailmen and occasionally knock on the doors of my grandmother's increasingly bemused neighbors, calling ourselves ethnographers and asking them to tell us about their people. Then we'd pretend to be Allison's parents. Those afternoons we stripped to our bathing suits, slathered ourselves with coconut tanning oil (though I was already browner than the woman on the bottle), and made over our faces with Allison's pilfered makeup kit. She swore her mother had so many cosmetics bags that she hadn't even noticed one was missing, something I found shocking, having a mother who practically considered ChapStick ornamental.

After our makeovers, Allison and I would climb to sit beside each other on a branch of the biggest tree above the lake, pretending it was a ship's deck, and the water beneath us the Atlantic Ocean. We imitated the way we'd heard adults talk, complained about our imaginary jobs, the scandalous behavior of our friends and coworkers, the way our families drove us crazy, and about—we never forgot this part—how much we missed our daughters and wished we'd taken them with us. I liked our pretend cruise ship days because I imagined us glamorous, like Allison's parents. When I pressed her for details about their travels, she'd just shrug, and say "How do I know? They never take me with them." I knew better than to say that my parents never took me with them, either, but they talked to me enough that I knew all about where they had been.

When our secret days were finished, we'd cool off by dipping our bodies in the shallow end of the lake, and then sneak back into my grandmother's house, dripping some combination of muddy lake water and suntan oil and high-end cosmetics across my grandmother's floors. On those occasions that Allison couldn't manage to charm forgiveness out of her, we accepted our increasingly restrictive punishments with some combination of amusement and grim determination: we cleaned bathroom tile with a toothbrush; we were not allowed to accompany my grandmother to the city on shopping trips; we ate Brussels sprouts for dinner for an entire week; we were spanked, which was new to both of us. My grandmother blamed me more than Allison for our expeditions.

Though we were equally guilty, I accepted the blame, knowing that whenever it was possible, whatever punishment she gave me

Allison would take along with me. Once we spent an entire morning locked in the bathroom. I'd been ordered not to come out until I had done something with my hair. We thought she was kidding us at first, because the door only locked from the inside anyway; but when we stopped laughing and tried to open it, we found she'd actually taken clothesline and looped it from the doorknob to the banister in order to shut us in. Originally it was supposed to be for an hour, but when she told me it wasn't even really a punishment, because a girl my age ought to be able to brush her own hair and it was a travesty that my mother hadn't taught me, I'd muttered that *she* couldn't even brush my hair, and look how old she was, and just like that one hour turned into six.

In the bathroom, Allison and I pretended that we'd been confined to our cruise ship cabins because of stormy conditions and choppy water. We sang "Kokomo" at the top of our lungs over and over again, and when that got old we ran the bathtub full of water and splashed each other until we were soaking, complaining that the storm was so bad our cabin was flooding. When my grandmother finally let us out, my hair looked the same as it had that morning, only damper. Insufficiently chastised, we collapsed at her feet giggling and shouting *Land! Land!* What did it matter, what chores she made us do or how many hours a day she forbade us to leave the house, when we had each other?

A month into the summer, my grandmother had a brainstorm. She sat us down in the family room after dinner one night, and told us that we absolutely must stop disobeying her and running off, that she'd become very worried about us, and that the next time we disappeared, she'd have no choice but to call the police. We nodded our assent, but were doubtful. Our grandmother had worried about what the neighbors would think when the gardener took a week off and *dandelions* had sprouted in her yard; we could only imagine what she'd do if people spotted a police car in her driveway. Sensing our skepticism, she leaned forward in her chair, looking first me and then Allison in the eyes.

"Do you know what's living in that lake?" our grandmother asked.

I thought we did. Minnows. Tadpoles. Mosquitoes we regularly slapped off of ourselves.

"Snakes," said my grandmother. "Snakes are in that lake."

I giggled. We'd seen the occasional small brown garden snake; my mother had told me before she left that there were a lot of them where she grew up, and I shouldn't be alarmed, because they were perfectly harmless. I repeated this to my grandmother.

"Tell your mother," said my grandmother, "that when you leave a place for twenty years, a lot changes. They've got these pythons that love water. Some idiots imported them as pets, and now they're taking over. A Burmese python can grow to be the size of the both of you put together, and can get you from twenty feet away. Sometimes they lay eggs in drainpipes, and the baby python will travel through the sewer pipes and come right in through a hole in a wall and eat their prey alive. When a python eats something it eats everything, even the bones. Crushes them completely. Lately there've been a lot of cats and dogs lost, even a huge Saint Bernard—vanished. I'd hate to lose a granddaughter. There'd be nothing left of you to find. Tell your mother she has never had any idea how easy it is for something to be destroyed."

Two weeks after that, I fell out of a bunk bed. My grandmother, sensing she'd gotten to me, had begun elaborating on the latest exploits of the Burmese python after dinner every night. A Burmese python had been caught in a child's bedroom in Orlando. A Burmese python had eaten an alligator in Lake Jackson; a tourist had gotten a picture of it happening, before he ran. A Burmese python came out of the pipes in a Miami kitchen; a plumber only narrowly escaped with his life, and only because he was too fat for the snake to get his jaws around. Three cats were missing from the house at the end of the block: they'd gone out in the morning as usual and simply never come back.

I consulted the books my parents had left me, contemplating metallurgy and purification rituals as forms of protection. Actually undertaking any of them was impossible, especially when I refused to leave the house. It wasn't just the outside world I was newly afraid of: I was haunted by what my grandmother had said about baby pythons, and imagined one growing and swelling inside the walls even now. My grandmother had won one battle—I stayed where she could see me, I tracked no more mud into her house—but she hadn't bargained for the way the fear would overtake me. I was afraid of snakes, yes, but I was also afraid of open windows, peeling paint, creaking floorboards, sinks, bathtubs, and toilets. I dropped the talisman I'd made out of the plastic wings and chewing gum down an open shower drain while trying to wash myself and hold it under the faucet at the same time. I refused to pee unless Allison held my hand, panicked when within ten feet of a wall, and tried my best not to sleep at night. One night, while trying to keep my body as far from the bedroom wall as possible, I fell from the top bunk. I hit my head, hard enough that it smacked sharply against the bare floor and Allison woke up screaming at the sound.

By the time my grandmother rushed into the room to see what had happened, Allison had already climbed out of the bottom bunk to sit beside me. My grandmother ran for her first, and I told myself, without believing it, that it was because she was the one who had screamed. Allison extracted herself from my grandmother's arms.

"Tara fell," she shrieked. "She fell off the top of the bed."

"Are you hurt?" my grandmother asked.

"I hit my head."

My grandmother pressed a palm to my forehead.

"You're not cut," she said. "Are you dizzy?"

I shook my head no.

"Don't move your head," said Allison, who had come by her medical knowledge through frequent viewings of her mother's favorite soap opera. "Grandma, she could have a concussion."

"The bed is five feet high," said my grandmother. "No one has a concussion. And if I take you to the hospital to find that out officially, they'd need to shave all those knots off the back of your head to see your scalp. Go back to bed, both of you. Come get me if you feel funny."

I didn't want to get back into the bed. I thought briefly that if I went to the hospital, my parents might be called and, upon hearing that the house had been overtaken by enormous pythons, come and get me out of here, maybe Allison too. But it was possible that no one would reach my parents. In any case, I believed my grandmother about the head shaving, and I didn't want to be bald. I stayed on the floor, thinking that the ground was a good safe distance from the walls and whatever might be inhabiting them. Allison's voice rescued me from the embarrassment of admitting I was afraid to get back into my bed. "I think," she announced with the authoritative wisdom of someone six months older, "you have a concussion. You shouldn't move. I'm going to sleep next to you so I can check your breathing."

She pulled the blue blanket off the bottom bunk and brought it to me. We curled up in the center of the floor, counting our breaths in whispers until they came almost in unison. I opened my eyes every few minutes to check the walls for any sign of movement, and check that Allison was still there. Every fourth or fifth time, I'd find Allison staring back at me, her two small fingers reaching out to feel the pulse on my neck.

By the next morning, I was jumpy again. I kept up my new rituals, persisted in refusing to go outside. Nightly, Allison persuaded me into our bedroom, letting me sleep in the bottom bunk with her. When I refused to even do that, she'd sleep beside me on the floor. I spent most of my days in the center of the living room. Among its advantages were a wall consisting almost entirely of plate glass windows, meaning there was one less direction from which I could be ambushed, and a wall of portraits that—once I'd read through the last of the books my parents had sent me with—I began to study in earnest, in order to keep myself entertained.

There was my grandmother's whole life, in gilded frames: the family together, my grandmother younger and undeniably beautiful, the grandfather I had never met. Pictures of my uncles as kids, their hair pressed down so flat it looked like they'd been wearing helmets before the pictures were taken. Uncle Mark and Uncle Timothy at high school and then college graduations. Wedding portraits, including one of Allison's father marrying his first wife. At the one Christmas dinner we'd spent together, my grandmother announced the first wife was a better woman than Allison's mother would ever be. Allison had run from the room in tears. Everyone else sat there like they hadn't heard her. My mother said later that if they'd all stopped eating every time my grandmother said something honest but awful, they would have starved to death before they were ten.

There were no pictures of my mother's wedding on my grandmother's wall. The pictures of her stopped at sixteen. There was my mother, wispy and young-looking, eyes wide open and surprised. I imagined her daydreaming before the photo was snapped. It wasn't long after that when my mother took off on a road trip across the country with friends who imagined themselves hippies. Some of these people were still my mother's friends, and in one of their houses I had seen pictures from that summer: my mother laughing and making faces in the backseat, my mother sleeping on a beach somewhere. My mother didn't talk about that summer. While she was off with her friends, my grandfather was killed when his small plane encountered a tropical storm and crashed.

In my grandmother's butterfly theory, my mother was the moth who flapped her wings in Japan and caused disaster; there was an inevitable correlation between her being in the wrong place at the wrong time and my grandfather's untimely accident. I had been given this secret knowledge too early to know what to do with it. I was old enough to know better than to prod my mother with questions, but too young to understand debt and obligation. Too young to understand what my mother must have felt during her mother's fight with cancer, or to appreciate the uncertainty my grandmother must have been living with. I was too young to understand that a python could be not just a threat but a warning, and too young to understand why this summer, of all summers, I had been sent off as a flawed peace offering.

Allison got impatient with my refusal to leave the living room. She tried to reason with me: "If a snake wanted to eat us, wouldn't it have done it already? If a starving python was living in our lake, wouldn't all the other animals be dead by now?" I wanted to believe her, but then I pictured myself being crushed into fine dust inside of something so big that no one could hear me scream, vanishing without my parents ever knowing what had happened. When logic failed, Allison retrieved my copy of *Natural Wonders of the Amazon Rain Forest* from where it lay abandoned and pointed out pictures of snake after snake.

"Look," she said, pointing at a picture of a man with a large yellow snake wrapped around his shoulders, two women in the background looking unphased. "All these people who live with snakes, and they haven't been eaten. Your parents are with these snakes right now, and they're not dead."

"How do you know?" I asked. They'd told me before leaving that by a month into the summer, they would be unreachable, leaving Rio for the dense territory of the rain forest, a place where they neither sent nor received letters.

Allison gave up on me after that. She stopped letting me sleep on the bottom bunk; she began to tease me about my fears. I made a new amulet out of one of Allison's barrettes and a friendship bracelet she had given me; Allison demanded the barrette back and, when I refused, ripped the bracelet in half. My phobia was taking a greater toll on her than boredom. Being inside meant she had to spend more time in the direct presence of my grandmother. My grandmother quizzed Allison incessantly about her grades, pulled her into the study to review brochures for day schools she wanted Allison to be prepared to apply to next summer. Allison's credentials sorely disappointed her; makeup theft and an active imagination were apparently not among the early markers of genius. Her grades were not great, and her school records were dotted with minor citations: Allison talked back to teachers, Allison poured glue in someone's hair, Allison stole the class turtle to keep as a pet. When I overheard my grandmother grilling Allison over these infractions, I shimmered with a kind of pride in her boldness, but Allison's explanations were alarmingly meek. Even my grandmother noticed that Allison seemed to get in some sort of trouble every time her parents left for a vacation, which they did often, year-round, but Allison refused to admit to the correlation.

My grandmother scheduled Allison for beginning piano lessons, and took her for informal conversations with a French-speaking neighbor. My grandmother didn't invite me to come, which saved me the trouble of refusing to leave with her. In any case, she wouldn't have had grounds to force me. My mother shared her views on language and music, if not her approach. I attended bilingual elementary school, and was in the school orchestra. Had she asked, my grandmother would have found out that I spoke fluent Spanish, and played the viola quite nicely.

There was a long time that I didn't talk about that summer at all, and then there were times when it was all I could talk about. It was the sort of thing that made a person interesting in college: My Youth as Real Live Tragic Mulatta. My recovery turned my scars into party favors. If you had seen them—the dot on my leg, the line on my elbow, the water in my eyes when I talked about Allison—then you had something about me to take with you. If you knew what was behind it, you had even more. *If you think your family was messed up,* people would whisper, *you should talk to that girl*. In my first year of law school I was famous for using myself as the basis for a sample torts question in study group. People wondered whether being so casual about it meant that I was screwed up, or that I was OK. I couldn't have answered them.

A confession: because I didn't know the difference between kinds of intimacy back then, I told each of the first four men I slept with that he was the only one I'd ever told this story. Jason was the fourth, and the only one to call me a liar: he'd already heard the story from my roommate the week before. According to him, it was part of what made him like me in the first place. I was so stunned that I kicked him out of bed and didn't speak to him again for months. But after he had left and I had given up trying to sleep, I wondered which part of the story had drawn him to me. I never asked, but I wondered. I wondered years later, when he called the Yale housing law clinic on behalf of the *New Haven Register* and, upon recognizing my name and voice at the other end of the line, asked me to dinner. I wondered—it was a tiny flash in the back of my mind, but yes, I wondered—when he brought me takeout during finals week at the end of my second year of law school, and I cracked open the fortune cookie and found an engagement ring. Was it the part of the story where I was strong that made me special, or the part where I was weak? It mattered more than I could say.

This is what I told him: My grandmother, it seems to me in retrospect, was a woman whose better impulses frequently led to her worst, the sort of person who would offer you a genuine favor, then punish you for having the gall not to take her up on it. The afternoon I ended up in the hospital, I think she started out meaning to help me.

"Look," she said, approaching me in the living room that day, bending down to my level to look me in the eye. "This is too much. You need to go outside today. I'm taking Allison swimming. You'll come with us."

"I don't swim anymore," I said. "Snakes like water."

"Be that as it may, they don't like chlorine. Go get your swimsuit on."

"No," I said. "I don't want to be eaten."

"Look," said my grandmother, exasperated, "it's possible that I *exaggerated* a little, so you would learn a lesson about running off. There *is* a Burmese Python, and they have spotted a few in the Everglades, but no one's ever heard of one this far north, and no one's ever heard of one eating an entire person, and the only dog missing around here is that Saint Bernard, who probably ran away because his owner is a fool and a drunk, and he may not even have stayed missing if she hadn't written her own damn phone number wrong on the lost dog poster. Get dressed."

"I don't believe you," I said.

"Why would I lie to you now?" she asked.

"Why would you lie to me about it in the first place?" I asked. "Either way, it makes you a liar. Maybe you just want me to get eaten."

"Don't you get smart with me," said my grandmother. "I never took lip from your mother and I certainly won't take it from you."

"Daddy says you took everything from my mother," I said, more innocently than was honest. There was a thick feeling in my throat.

My grandmother's eyes narrowed. She was silent for some minutes. When she left the room I could hear my breath coming rapidly in tune with her retreating then returning footsteps. In the moment I first saw the gleam of metal in her hand, I truly believed she was going to stab me.

She never said a word. She started snipping quickly, unevenly, the rhythm of her anger punctuated by the growing pile of tight black curls on the floor. It didn't occur to me to run. It didn't occur to me that there was anywhere to go. I don't know how long Allison had been watching. I only know that when it was over, and all but half an inch of my shoulder-length-when-it-lay-flat hair was piled on the floor, Allison was in the doorway, looking straight at my grandmother.

She walked over to me and grabbed my hand, dragging me toward the front door. I didn't know what to believe about snakes anymore, but at that moment I would have preferred being inside a python's belly to seeing my grandmother look at my practically bald head like she had proved something to me. I followed Allison down to our lake, climbed with her to the top of our tree. We were out of stories, or we were out of words. We didn't pretend to be my mother in the Amazon, or hers on a cruise ship, because we knew what we were right then: people too small to stop the things we didn't want to happen from happening anyway. The bottoms of my jeans and Allison's thin ankles were muddy then, our socks wet from a puddle I could not remember having stepped in. I looked down before I remembered not to. I saw our watery reflections blending into one on the water's wet canvas, pink and peach and beige and denim softly swirling, and wondered how my grandmother managed to see two of us so clearly.

"I want to go home," Allison said. "I want us to run away. I hate that woman."

"She likes you," I said.

"If she liked me, she'd like you too. You're my best friend."

"No I'm not," I said, and realized as I said it that something about the last few weeks had made it true.

Then I saw Allison's reflection lift her arms, felt the weight of her palms on my back, felt myself rock forward. In those first few seconds, I could feel the fall in my belly, a sharp reminder of gravity, the constancy of the laws of physics even when they run counter to everything else we'd have ourselves believe in. We are safe, with our families, until we are not. On the way down, I remembered dropping out of the bunk bed, thought about how much worse the first moment of the fall had been than the actual impact. I braced myself for the slap of the water, but was still unprepared for the sting of it against my nostrils, the sharpness of the underwater rock on which I landed.

I woke up in a hospital room with blue walls. It was not my mother cradling my head and humming but my aunt Claire, who, as always, had soft hands and smelled like peach lotion. She was much thinner than she'd been two months ago: for the first time I believed she was as sick as my mother had said and felt the sharp stab of what I could finally name as anger fade a bit. Aunt Claire apologized to me nonetheless. "If I had known," she said over and over again, "what kind of people they were leaving you with, I would have insisted you stay with me." Allison had admitted what she'd done, and my aunt Claire had already dismissed my grandmother from the premises, told the nurses she was not allowed in my hospital room, though I couldn't exactly see her trying to sneak in.

The department chair had located my parents, who were on their way home. I spent a few days in the hospital looking, between the piles of blankets well-intentioned nurses kept putting on my bed and the scratchy blue paper hospital gown, worse than I actually felt. Help had arrived quickly enough that there hadn't been much water in my lungs. I had scraped up an arm pretty badly, and knocked myself unconscious with some combination of fear and impact, but the worst of my injuries was a broken tibia. Once the wound above it closed and the risk of infection passed, the doctors told me it would heal normally. Though my leg occasionally throbbed, and the cast I wore itched like crazy, I reminded myself that I was lucky. I'd over-heard a doctor telling my aunt that if the rock had hit my head two inches lower, the fall would have killed me.

Aunt Claire stayed in a Tallahassee hotel until my parents got back, visiting and reading me kids' books. I was too exhausted to pretend I was too old for them. She made me excited promises about all the things we could do with my hair when it started to grow back, and was always reluctant to leave me for the hotel in the evening. I turned nine in the hospital; a nurse baked me a homemade red velvet cake; the entire pediatric staff sang to me; Aunt Claire bought me a beautiful set of turquoise-jeweled hair combs to decorate my shorter hair.

When my mother finally arrived, I heard her before I saw her. My parents had gotten in at midnight and come straight to the hospital. It was one in the morning when they got there, four days after my admittance, and they had to threaten several overprotective nurses in order to be allowed to wake me. When my mother saw me, she cried. My father was so wrapped up in hugging me and so close to crying himself that I don't know if he even noticed her tears, but I wished somebody would have held her.

"I'm so sorry, baby," she said when she had composed herself. "We never should have left you. Allison is damn lucky she called the cops, lucky you're alive, and lucky your father and I don't believe in juvenile detention centers, or we'd be pressing charges against her for pushing you off in the first place."

"Maybe it was just an accident," I said. What I meant was that Allison might have wanted to go home, more than she wanted to hurt me. Hadn't she said so? Hadn't she confessed, even before I was awake to accuse her?

My mother waved this possibility off.

"I called my brother," she said. "They cut their cruise short in Guam and came back several days ago. She's got a lot of problems that have nothing to do with you. She's very confused. This is all your grandmother's doing. I'm sure if she hadn't been treating you so badly, Allison wouldn't have thought she could do the same. Why didn't you tell me what was going on in that house?"

I considered this. *I* was very confused.

"You were in Brazil," I said finally. "What are they going to do to Allison now?"

"Frankly, that's her parents' problem now, not mine," said my mother, cradling me closer to her, and stroking my still naked feeling head. "My only job is to take care of you."

But Allison was the other half of the story; the half I didn't tell because it didn't belong to me anymore. People would ask me sometimes what happened to her. "I'm sure she grew up," I would say, and they would nod at my empathy and rarely point out that *growing up* did not mean and never has meant the same thing as *getting better*. The truth was I didn't know much about how Allison was doing. My mother had deliberately cut off contact with her family after that summer, deciding the whole lot of them were toxic. I'd heard her though, talking to my father about the fact that my uncle had decided to leave Allison with my grandmother for a little while, to straighten her out. "That's a mistake," my mother had said. "What an unfortunate pair."

An unfortunate pair. Her words were in the back of my mind when she called me a few weeks after my law school graduation. I had been hibernating, wearing headphones and reviewing for the Connecticut bar, and it was only because she called three times in a row that I bothered to pick up the phone.

"Tara," my mother said, "the first thing I want you to know is you don't have to do this."

"OK . . ." I said.

"Allison is in the hospital," she said.

"What's wrong with her?" It occurred to me, stupidly, that maybe she needed a kidney.

"She tried to kill herself," my mother said.

"My God," I said.

"She's asked to see you," my mother said. "Apparently, her therapist thinks it would be good for her to talk to you. I'm sure she wants to apologize in person. But I told them, you have a life, too, and we'll do this on your schedule, if at all, OK?"

"I'll do it," I said.

My mother paused on the other end of the line.

"I'll book us flights," she said finally.

"I can go by myself," I said.

"No you can't," she said. "I don't trust those people with you for a second."

Her fear was understandable, if belated. The year after my summer with *the unfortunate pair*, I didn't sleep more than an hour a night. When I said so later, my mother said that wasn't biologically possible, and then changed the subject. My father said it simply wasn't true, because he didn't sleep well that year and he remembers waking up nights, walking down the hall, and pulling back the blankets in my room to check on me. "You slept," he told me, "like an angel." Perhaps they are right. When I was very little, my mother used to say there was something of my grandmother in me, in how I tell stories the way I need them to be and not the way that they actually happened. In any case, I remember staring at the ceiling every night for a year, tracing shadow patterns with my finger. I remember closing my eyes whenever I heard footsteps outside the door and relaxing every time I realized it was only my father.

My parents were careful with me like they'd never been before; I was in college before they were willing to let me out of their sight for more than a few hours. Even when Aunt Claire requested my company, to sit beside her bed and read to her those last few months before she died, they were reluctant to part with me. That summer was still with me somewhere, and so was Allison, and my grandmother, but thinking about any of it was like looking at an old photograph of myself, staring a long time and all the while trying to figure out whether it was really me in the picture.

And then there I was in Tallahassee again, this time in a downtown mental institution, only the kind with a marble lobby and a fountain on the grounds, so you were supposed to call it a wellness center. I had waited for my mother's flight at the airport and had lunch with her when she landed. Though she insisted on driving me to see Allison, she announced in the parking lot that it was probably best if she not come in, and I agreed with her. The grounds of the wellness center reminded me of the grounds of the country club so long ago. Everything was flowering, in obstinate resistance to the severity of its locale.

When I announced who I was and whom I'd come to see, the woman behind the desk looked at me sharply for a second but then looked again, nodded, and told me I had my grandmother's eyes. A nurse in a powder blue uniform escorted me down the hall to a waiting area with plush teal chairs. I sat in one of them before I even took note of who was sitting on the other end of the room. My grandmother looked older, of course—her hair now gone completely white, her face creased with wrinkles—but there was no mistaking her. Her eyes were still as sharp as ever, her mouth still set in a line of grim determination. Her wardrobe, though, was in a state of disarray, her silk scarf tossed on the chair beside her, her blouse and pants wrinkled as though she had been sleeping in them—which, I supposed, was entirely possible. She looked at me, gave me an almost smile. I tried to think of a comforting thing to say to her, the kind of thing you would say to a stranger in similar circumstances, but nothing came to mind. I focused instead on the insulting giddiness of the waiting-room magazine covers, their cheerful refusal to be about anything that mattered.

A nurse punctuated the silence. "Miss Ellis?"

She led me down the hallway and opened the door to a room, but didn't enter. I could see her hovering in the entry. Before I walked through the door, I heard Allison's voice, still thick like sweet liquid. "You came."

She looked worse than I was expecting, but I already couldn't remember how I'd pictured her all this time. Certainly I was never picturing her in a hospital bed, with bandages and an IV and a red plastic food tray in her lap. She was thinner now than she had been when I had known her as a child; the roundness I remembered in her face had given way to something angular. Her eyes, which I'd remembered as being almost electric blue, seemed gray in this light, and her long hair was feathered with split ends. She looked exposed in a flimsy cloth gown; I wondered if there were levels of crazy here, if some people qualified to wear real clothes and others didn't. I closed my eyes, then opened them again. Allison smiled at me. I smiled back. I looked around the room, wondering what was coming next. The clock on the wall ticked loudly, as if counting down for an explosion.

"What happened?" I asked, which was the most delicate way I could think of putting the question. Something cold flashed through her eyes briefly, and then she smiled at me again. "I got divorced last month," she said. "But I got divorced once before, and I didn't try to kill myself afterward, so I guess that's not it, is it?"

"I'm sorry," I said.

"I probably should have learned my lesson about marriage the first time."

"Thanks for the warning." I nodded at my engagement ring.

"I bet he's a nice guy," Allison said. "Is he a lawyer too?"

"Jason's a journalist," I said. "And I'm not a lawyer yet. I just graduated."

"Still, look at you now. I always hoped you were doing well. Our grandmother would love it."

The way she said it, it sounded like an accusation and a compliment at the same time. I waited for her to tell me why she'd asked me to come. To fill the silence, I told her a little about school, about Jason, about the sample bar question essays I'd written out and read into a tape recorder that I played so often I could hear it in my sleep.

"What are you doing these days?" I asked finally.

"Other than slitting my wrists?"

I flinched.

"I teach music," she said. "We tried to make a real pianist out of me, but I was never quite good enough. My heart wasn't in it."

"'We'?"

"Grandma and I," she said. "Grandma more than me. My parents gave me to her after that summer, you know. They put me in a place like this for a few weeks, and when I came out they said they simply *lacked the knowledge* to deal with a child with those kinds of issues. They moved to LA the next year."

"I know," I said. I had known, but hearing it out loud still felt like a slap. "I never understood why you told them. You could have said I'd fallen. I never told them you pushed me. I never said that. I wouldn't have."

"I could have said a lot of things," said Allison. "I thought my parents would come get me and yours would come get you. I thought if anyone got in trouble, it would be our grandmother."

"I'm sorry," I said. "We were kids. We didn't know what we were doing."

"It took me all these years to figure out that she didn't know, either. She had the next decade of my life scheduled before my parents were on the plane. She was so scared to mess up again that I was barely allowed to leave the house. I think I got married the first time just to get away from her. She went on and on about my first husband being trash. Her favorite thing to say when I messed up was that I took after my mother's side of the family, and water seeks its level. I guess it never occurred to her I hadn't seen my mother in years, or that it probably didn't say much about her that I had decided that moving into a trailer with a man who sold cheap souvenirs in the Everglades would have been better than going back to her house."

"But you went back," I said.

"I didn't know where else to go. So I lived with her until I got married again last year. He was grandmother-approved, but that didn't stop him from sleeping with our next-door neighbor. Maybe I would have been better off staying in the Everglades. Lots of snakes there, but most of them are harmless. Sometimes seeing one would startle me, and I would think of you."

I closed my eyes. I thought about all the things I'd accumulated since I'd last seen Allison, and how absolutely useless they seemed right now.

"Maybe you just need to start over someplace new," I said. "Get away from all of this. You could stay with me for a while when they let you out."

She parted her lips a little, like she was going to laugh, but she didn't. I tried to picture it in my head: the look on Jason's face when I told him I was bringing home a suicidal white woman who had almost killed me once; Jason and I converting the study into a bedroom for her, getting a piano, her getting settled in Connecticut. I imagined our kids growing up together, the way she and I had thought we would.

"Maybe I'd like that," she said finally. "I never thought of you getting married without me. Remember, we were going to be each other's bridesmaid?"

"I remember," I said. "I was going to pick mint green dresses, because that was your favorite color, and you were going to pick orange, because it was mine. Jason's sister is being a pain in the neck and doesn't want to wear the dress I picked out. You should be a bridesmaid instead. I'd even change the color for you."

"You would," she said. "But I just wanted to see you. I just wanted you to see me. Take care of yourself. I really am glad you're happy."

I looked at the clock again, then back at Allison. It had been an hour; I was ready to go, though still uneasy about why I'd been sent for in the first place. I reached for her hand and squeezed it by way of good-bye. She didn't ask me to stay. I felt like somebody ought to stop me from walking out, like there was a rule that you couldn't leave behind such palpable need.

In the waiting room, my grandmother still sat. I was struck by how open she looked, the way her grief pulled her out of herself the way most people's tucks them in. I felt bigger than her for the first time in my life, but I couldn't feel good about it. I thought of saying something to her, but I didn't know where to start, how to explain who I was now, or what she'd had to do with it.

"I hear you're really something these days," she said when I stopped in front of her. "Congratulations."

"Thank you," I said, before I had time to regret it. I turned my back to leave, waited for her to say something else. I only heard her breathing.

My mother was still in the car outside. When I knocked on the window to be let in, she jumped, then seemed relieved to see it was me.

"I'm sorry you had to do that," she said as I got in the car. "You're a better person than I'd be, in your shoes."

"I'm not," I said. "It wasn't a big deal. It was a long time ago."

" 'A long time ago'— Tara, we almost lost you. Maybe you don't remember, but to me it's like yesterday. Like yesterday."

"How could you possibly remember?" I said. "You weren't there."

The tone of my own voice surprised me. My mother looked stung and I was sorry, but not sorry enough to apologize. She bit back tears.

"Tara, don't. I mean, not now. Look, I wanted you to have your own life and me to have mine. I made a mistake, putting you there that summer. But I loved you, you always knew I loved you?"

I didn't think she meant for it to be a question, so I didn't answer her directly.

"I didn't mean it like that."

I looked out the window, watching people at a park through the glass. I thought of saying a lot of things that I didn't. I didn't tell her how badly I had wanted her back, not just that summer, but all the years before it; how those days she had lain beside me in the hospital bed, for once mine and mine alone, were among the best of my childhood. I didn't tell her that every time I took note of the scar on my elbow, I thought she ought to thank me for giving her the way out of her mother's house that she'd never found for herself, no matter how many times she ran away. I didn't tell her how I had learned it wasn't just snakes that could eat you alive. I didn't tell her what I had told no one in all these years, what I had lied about even to the love of my life, because saying it out loud would unravel so much. Whatever motives Allison had for saying so—whatever she thought she saw a way out of, or more likely, back into, in confession—there had been no push, no one's hands on my back. I hadn't fallen, I'd jumped. It was shallow water, and though as it turned out I'd been lucky not to kill myself, at the time it hadn't seemed like a long way down. Twenty feet and I would have my parents back, I would have my mother forever, I would have years before I had to consider the costs. I'd been, for the second time that summer, less afraid of the fall than what else I thought awaited me. That afternoon above the murky water, which I remembered quite clearly, there had been nothing but me, looking down at my own reflection, and seeing at last a way toward what I wanted most.

Harvest

ggs. They wanted eggs, and their requests came trickling in daily in ten-point type, through the want ads of the campus paper. Five, ten, fifteen thousand you could get for doing it just once. More than that if you were experienced. We knew girls who did it over and over and over again, once a semester. Mostly they were girls whose parents paid their full tuition anyway, and the money quickly manifested itself as stuff: cashmere sweaters crumpled on the bathroom floor, new stilettos clicking across the kitchen linoleum, matchboxes from Le Cirque and Nobu, endless overpriced trinkets collected on excursions to the East Side. Sometimes the stuff was more practical: new computers, a savings account for grad school. Sometimes it was just bigger: a brand-new entertainment center that got stolen the next week, and shame on us, because we weren't particularly sorry when it did.

It wasn't our eggs they wanted, so we spent the weekends watching burned DVDs and chasing ramen noodles with Corona the way broke college students were supposed to. Columbia credentials be damned, no one was interested in paying us for our genetic material. If they had wanted brown babies who so obviously didn't belong to them, they would have just adopted. Laura Kelso, who lived in our suite—that was whose eggs they wanted. I was surprised no one had come to our door to recruit her personally; she'd practically stepped out of a want ad. 1600 SAT score, 4.1 GPA, and that only because some professors didn't believe in A+'s. Then, of course, there was the important stuff: blonde, blue-eyed, five-foot-seven, barely 115 pounds, though we suspected the green pills she stored in a clear plastic bottle with the label torn off were diet pills of some kind. She'd been normal-sized when we met her.

She was making bank, but we couldn't hate her for it. Absent her new income, she would have been broke like the rest of us: too good a daughter to guilt her single mother into sending more money than she could afford. Laura's mother was a cashier at Penney's; what she could afford wasn't much. For a while that had given us a claim to her. She was a homegirl, a *hermanita*: we were in this together. Then she walked through the front door wearing Jimmy Choo boots, and we knew we were losing her. Before we knew it, we hardly saw her, and then one day she invited Ellen Chambers, serial donor, and Lisette Hartley, serial bitch, into our common area for some egg donor support group, and they compared paychecks and pain levels and wondered what had become of the little pieces of them released into the universe. We sat in Candy's room with the door open and faked gagging. Nicole let the back pages of *The Village Voice* fall open, 900 numbers and round brown asses staring up at us from the floor. She said, "They're *mother* material, but who wants to fuck them? If we were hookers, we'd be making twice what they were."

We did not particularly want to be hookers, and so this was little consolation.

What we wanted was to be a doctor, a lawyer, a spy, and happy. Nicole was the aspiring doctor; she had a love-hate relationship with her bio texts, but a love-love relationship with catalogues of all kinds. Pinned to her wall where Mos Def and Che Guevara hung on ours were ads for designer shoes and clothing, electronic equipment— even the occasional house ripped out of the home buyer's guide to remind her of the bigger picture, the things she'd wanted growing up but never had. Candy wanted to be a lawyer: she had big ideas about justice and was always dragging us to meetings with her, hoping we'd pick up some of her conviction. Truth be told, Candy could have been Laura Kelso's dark-haired sister, but we didn't dare say so. Freshman year at a sisterhood meeting, some girl had looked at Candy walking in and sneered, not quite under her breath, "What the hell is white girl doing here?" Not three seconds later, Candy was all in her face, like: "*Mira*, my people did not get half exterminated and have half their country stolen from them for you to be calling me a white girl, OK, bitch?" You didn't mess with Candy; she was going to be one scary-ass lawyer.

Me, I wanted to be the spy. I liked secrets. Nicole, ever the realist, liked to point out that spies couldn't be spies on their own behalf, and I had yet to encounter a government or revolution of which I approved. So far I had not accepted the seriousness of this problem. I didn't like to think about the future, and we were only juniors, so I didn't quite have to. Courtney was the one who said she just wanted to be happy. Nicole said this was her middle-class showing. Courtney was from one of those barely middle-class black families where the girls are always called Courtney or Kelli or Lindsay or Brooke, and the family forgoes vacations and savings and stock for a nice house in a nice neighborhood in the hopes that the neighbors will forget they are black. Usually what happened was Kelli tried so hard to prove her parents right that she turned into a bleach-blonde, rock-music-loving creature who seemed foreign to them. Lindsay got so tired of being called white girl that she studied Ebonics on BET and started dressing like a video extra, calling herself Lil L, and begging to hang out in the neighborhood they'd moved out of. Brooke, sick of not fitting in, would become anorexic or suicidal or both. We were all proud of Courtney for coming to us relatively normal.

Laura faded from us gradually. We kept our doors shut and she began to keep hers closed as well. We didn't know whether this was in retaliation or because she wasn't interested in hanging out with us. We never heard her in the shower, we rarely heard her enter: she seemed to glide. It was like we lived with a ghost—a snowflake, Nicole called her, and though she meant it in the harshly disapproving vein with which we spoke of most girls who were pale and delicate and seemed to be everywhere, in a more gentle sense the word had a ring of truth to it. We were living with something barely visible, something that might have vanished any second.

. . .

In tenth grade, I went through a bad-romance-novel phase. In bad romance novels, women always know the moment they are pregnant; the heroine can feel her lover plant his seed inside her, or something equally melodramatic. Perhaps because I subconsciously expected pregnancy to announce itself with some such motherly feeling of omniscience, I completely overlooked mine. Winter gave way to spring, and when I started getting queasy, I thought maybe I was lactose intolerant. When quitting dairy didn't help, I thought maybe I had an ulcer. Nicole, Candy, and Courtney started to notice something was off, but by the nature of their prying questions, I could tell they were thinking I was bulimic. It wasn't until I was lying on the floor, listening to Candy complain that her cramps were killing her, that I realized I hadn't had my period for two months. It had never been regular and I had grown accustomed to red spots on my underwear at odd intervals. There was something almost thrilling about its off-kilter arrival. I liked surprises. When my friends swallowed little green and white and blue pills and marked the start date of their periods on calendars, I thought how boring it must be to have your body run like clockwork. Turning sideways and inhaling bits of dust off Courtney's carpet, I understood that my dislike of the pill was irrational, but it was too late for all that.

Of course I had a boyfriend. We all did, they were like accessories; we kept them stored at colleges up and down the East Coast and pulled them out on formal occasions or in the event of extreme boredom or loneliness. Mine I kept at NYU, where he was lonely more than I was. I had spent a good number of nights downtown, curled up in his blue flannel sheets, listening to him breathe. He was good at hand-holding and being subtly witty and distracting me when I was on the verge of tears, brilliant in that completely useless way where he could tell you off the top of his head the architect of any office building downtown and the historic relationship between the toothbrush and cultural imperialism, but not what day of the week it was or what train to take to where. I didn't want to see him yet, so I bought a pregnancy test to confirm what I already knew, and then another in case the first one had been wrong, and then I threw the two sticks with their faint plus signs into the trash can and called my mother.

People who do not call my mother "Mother" call her Isis. Her name conjures up a persona that she indulges with miniature altars and smoky incense when she is not busy being a hairdresser. She was not busy at all when I called, the vague hum of her meditation music in the background let me know that.

"Angel. I was just thinking of you."

Every time I call my house, even those times when I am calling because my mother has forgotten to pick me up or call me back or send me something necessary, she tells me she has just been thinking of me. I ignored her and started talking, hoping maybe with some small talk she would pick up on the tremor of my voice. I was lying on the bed in my underwear when I called her, pinching the fat at my abdomen and trying to determine whether there was more of it, looking down at my breasts and wondering if they were any bigger.

I looked the same to me. I wondered if maybe I was imagining this. Stupid girls got pregnant, careless girls, girls who didn't worry about their futures, girls whose mothers had never explained to them about sex.

Laura had been a girl something like that when she'd come to college—not stupid, but naive, uninformed. She'd been sitting in the back row of the mandatory safe-sex lecture, wide-eyed, when we met her. They'd divided us into teams and made us do races to put a condom on a banana and she'd screwed it up, put the thing on backward and had it go flying off somewhere, then blushed a brilliant shade of red and hid her face in her hands. The girls on the other team laughed.

"It's OK," Nicole said, putting a hand on her shoulder after we lost. "There are too many hos on this campus anyway. Who comes to college knowing how to put a condom on in five seconds?"

"Don't say 'hos,'" said Candy. "Just 'cause somebody likes sex doesn't make her a ho."

They argued all the way to the dining hall while Laura and Courtney and I exchanged hellos and shy smiles.

Nicole and Candy were virgins then, too, though you wouldn't have known it by looking at them. Even on budgets they knew how to dress like city girls, girls who knew their way around—not like Laura, whose wardrobe screamed Kmart and favored the color pink. Maybe that was why we'd liked her right away: her need for us was immediately apparent, and unlike most of the people who needed us, we knew what to do for her.

I told my mother about Nicole's new Triple Five Soul sweatshirt and Candy's plans to go abroad next year. Pages rustled in the background. My mother told me how Mrs. Wilson from down the street thinned all her hair out, leaving braids in too long.

"She'll be back by Easter," my mother said. "She won't let anybody else do her hair for Easter Sunday."

"Uh-huh," I started to agree, but my mother had already interrupted herself to read out loud from the catalogue she was thumbing through. Health crystals, mood-balancing jewelry, a guide to spiritual belly dancing.

"Spiritual belly dancing, Angel. Doesn't that sound like fun?"

I imagined myself dancing for a minute, and then I imagined my belly fat, swollen, with stretch marks, and felt most unspiritual. I told her I had a test to study for.

"OK," she conceded. "You should go out later, though. Your horoscope says it's a good day for Pisces to be in the right place at the right time."

I hung up and thought to myself that the right place was two months ago in Rafael's bedroom, but I wasn't sure what my horoscope could do about that.

In the morning I skipped a review session and took the C train to Brooklyn to visit my father. He opened the door to my still-raised fist and seemed pleasantly surprised to see me.

"Angel. To what do I owe the honor, Miss Lady?"

My father had called me Miss Lady since I was four years old, and though I had not been prissy enough to deserve the nickname since then, it stuck. Uncomfortably, dishonestly, but it stuck. I walked in without answering his question. My visits were always like this. I liked to disrupt him. Interrupting people was the only way I could be sure of my presence in their lives.

My father's apartment had been painted red since the last time I was in it. I could still smell the newness of the paint. It looked as though he had painted it himself; whoever did it had forgotten a drop-cloth, and the furniture was flecked with red.

"Better not let the cops in here, Daddy. They'll think you killed someone."

He didn't hear me. Instead, I heard the pop of two bottle tops and then he walked into the living room and handed me a soda. My father drank only the kind that came in glass bottles; he believed aluminum was unhealthy, and wouldn't drink or eat anything that came out of a can.

"I want you to hear something," he said, before I had a chance to open my mouth. I occupied myself by running my tongue around the rim of the bottle. My father had his back to me and was messing with the ancient stereo in the corner of his living room.

My father was into radio then. My father was always into something; he was a collector of hobbies and habits. Sometimes I wondered how my parents could have been in the same room for long enough to conceive me, let alone be married for four years, but my mother had amassed her own fair share of collections over the years. I imagined their marriage was just a phase during which they had collected each other until something more interesting came along. A year ago my father was into the stock market, but then he invested the few hundred dollars he'd made initially in a company that marketed giant tomatoes, and lost it all. Now he planned to get famous doing radio commercials.

The tape started. I watched its wheels spin as my father's buttery baritone echoed out of the brown speakers, their wood paneling peeling at the edges. In two minutes of tape, my father sounded convincing selling: cars, liquor, a swanky restaurant downtown. He sounded unconvincing selling: study aids, season tickets for the Knicks, diet pills. He sounded downright ridiculous selling: golfing equipment, stain remover, the *Daily News*.

"What do you think, Miss Lady?" he asked when the tape stopped.

I said, "Daddy, I'm pregnant."

My father said nothing, finished his soda in a few sips, and rested it on top of the speaker. He left the room and I heard creaking in the kitchen, the squeak of hinges, and then the rustling of cabinet clutter. He emerged triumphantly, smiling, and handed me a sticky, half-gone bottle of molasses.

"Take a spoonful of this every day, it's good for the baby. Your mother took it when she was pregnant, and look how good you turned out."

From the looks of the dusty amber thing he had just handed me, the letters on its label faded into nonexistence, my mother had taken her spoonfuls from that very same bottle.

"I might not keep it," I said.

"Oh." He looked uncomfortable, as though he wondered why I

was telling him this. It was simple. I had screwed up, I wanted to punish somebody. He sat beside me on the couch and held my hand.

"Whatever you think is best, baby. You were always the smart one."

The smart one. That was my other nickname growing up. It was only recently that I had been able to convince people it didn't necessarily apply, either. I got up.

"I gotta go, Daddy. I'll call you."

I walked quickly and let the door slam on his parting fatherly advice.

I wanted to hurt somebody, and so far it wasn't working. My mother, when all was said and done and she finally found out, would be devastated that she hadn't been the first to know, but I couldn't even have that yet. I went to see Rafael not so much because I thought he should know as because he was woundable.

Rafael is an artist, in the most clichéd college-student, nude-self-portraits-on-the-wall kind of way. There are also nude pictures of me on his wall, though I am not identifiable in any of them—an elbow here, a belly button there, an arched brow, the curve of my thigh. The one with my breasts is in his portfolio but didn't make the wall. "I don't want other guys staring at my girlfriend's tits," he said. He does not, however, mind people looking at the picture of his penis he has pasted to the ceiling, though he did take it down when his little sister came to visit.

Rafael was raised in Miami by Catholic parents who left Cuba just before Castro came to power. His father did work for the

League of Cuban Voters, his mother was the president of an anti-Castro society and the most respected woman in the church that he attended twice every Sunday until he left for school. He started sleeping with me the same week that he took down the family portrait beside his bed and replaced it with a photo of Castro. I was not stupid enough to believe this was coincidence. I imagined him on the phone with his mother: *No, I'm not a virgin anymore and maybe Castro was right about you and do you know what else, Ma, she's black, even darker brown than Grandma Margarita, what are you going to do to me now?*

Probably this conversation never happened. I didn't particularly care if it did. I rather relished being his own personal Eve. It felt reckless and romantic. When I played I Never with my cousins over winter break, they raised impressed eyebrows when I drank to both *Have you ever devirginized somebody?* and *Have you ever done it with a Catholic?* People thought I was the good kid, but going to college was pretty much the only thing I'd done that they hadn't.

Now, though, confronted with Rafael, I would have traded all my good grades to know what to say to him. I had gone there to hurt him without knowing that I wasn't capable of it. He rambled about how we really only had to be part-time next year to finish and we could get an apartment somewhere uptown and he'd just take the train to class and we'd get summer jobs to save money, floundering when he tried to be more specific and making grossly obvious mathematical errors when he tried to compute our budget in his head. He was adorable and lost and I wanted to hold him until he felt better, but then I realized I was the one in trouble.

"Rafael, shut up," I said.

"I love you," he said. It was almost an afterthought.

I could hear the subtext to it, the desperate chord underneath. I love you. I love you enough. But I knew what enough turned into. One day you could have enough, and the next you had a house full of mood crystals or an apartment full of the sound of your own voice in stereo.

"I don't think I'm keeping it," I told him.

"Angel," he said, then stopped. I could see him struggling. We'd had this conversation before, in the theoretical sense. For most of his life he'd been told that abortion was a mortal sin, that to even let a girl do it was to shirk his responsibility as a man and a Christian. Those voices echoed somewhere deep, somewhere I had never been. Then there were the more recent voices: his newly declared agnosticism that called those other voices archaic and self-righteous; the voices that asked who was he to ever tell a woman what to do with her body, as though he were the boss of her. He had been told so much and become so accustomed to his own opinion not mattering that at the critical moment he seemed not to know what his own thoughts on the matter were and couldn't finish his sentence. Or maybe it had nothing to do with that. Maybe it was just him being selfish the way that most artists are, part drawn to the idea of something that would outlast him, part worried that he couldn't control it.

"Angel," he said again.

Usually when I found myself not knowing what to say to make things better, I kissed him instead. If it were anything else he was upset about, I'd be undoing the buttons on his shirt and kissing circles down his chest until the distressing moment was gone, our fingers in each other's hair, across each other's bodies. I would lie beneath him and raise my hips to meet his while he breathed into the curve of my neck and kept a hand cupped under my butt. I would bite his earlobe and think *I love this boy* and Fidel would watch the whole thing silently. Then it would be over and we would breathe heavily and know where we were wounded but not how to make it better.

Instead, I left, and told him I'd call him once I thought about it. I wouldn't, though; I decided the least I could do was make him call me. I returned to the dorm to find the girls sprawled across the common-area furniture and thought maybe they would do. It was midterm reading week, but no one was actually reading. My friends were eating chips and salsa while an underfed starlet railed against the injustice of life on MTV, buzzing in low volume while Nicole talked over it.

"You know what Laura has now?" she asked.

Value, I thought, but said nothing.

"Some damn two-hundred-dollar jeans. Can you believe? I'm about to donate me an egg."

"Please, girl. Who you gonna find wants a Nicole egg?" Candy said.

"Well, then you're about to haul your light ass in there and donate an egg, then cut me a percent." Nicole continued, "Twenty seems fair. Could get me some cute jeans anyway."

"Right. Let me go in there and sign Dulce Maria Gutierrez Hernandez on the dotted line and see how fast they throw me out the office. Who knows what could be hiding in DNA with a name like that. Maybe the kid would only get a 1400 and its whole life would be over." Candy laughed. I felt sick. Nicole kept going.

"Well, there gotta be some rich-ass black people who can't have their own kids and think my 1500's worth something. C'mon, Courtney, your parents got money, right? Think they want another kid? A better one?"

Courtney threw a lime Tostito at Nicole. I walked away without them noticing and tried to imagine telling them. Nicole would say to be realistic. She'd go through numbers the way Rafael had tried to, only hers would add up and show how ridiculous the situation would be. She'd tell me we didn't come this far to screw it up now. Candy would say it was only guilt keeping me from doing what had to be done right now, and then she'd go on a tangent about the government's attempts to restrict female sexuality, and when I was about to walk away and she realized what she was doing she'd apologize and then have nothing left to say. Courtney would just keep asking what I wanted, which wouldn't be any more helpful than me asking my damn self.

I knocked on Laura's door, not sure what I wanted from her. She looked startled to see it was me knocking; it had been months since we'd had a real conversation. We'd spoken only in passing, when at all: hello, cold today, isn't it, psych midterm's going to be a real pain in the ass.

"What do you want?" she asked, not quite rudely but headed there.

"Can I come in?" I said. "I need to talk."

Maybe she could tell it was serious, because she opened the door all the way and moved aside so that I could enter. Her first few checks had mainly gone to her mother, to paying off her loans, but the last one she'd clearly spent redecorating. The cheap navy comforter had been replaced by something purple and woven. *Egyptian cotton*, I thought, without knowing where the term had come from. The photos on her walls were not of us anymore; they were of her at clubs I'd never been to with girls I didn't recognize. Her pajamas were screaming Nick & Nora and her hair had recently been highlighted, and I had to look at the floor in order to pretend she was the same girl I'd once been friends with, the girl who couldn't say "Blow Pop" because she thought it sounded dirty, the girl who'd been confused about how it was possible to pee while wearing a tampon before Nicole broke it down for her. I told her the whole story, with the vomiting and the not knowing and my mother's health crystals and my father's car commercials, and Rafael being all beautiful and tortured and useless. She nodded in a kind of horrified sympathy, and then asked:

"What do you need me to do?"

I needed her to stop looking at me. I needed her eyes to not be blue and liquid. I needed her to understand what she couldn't possibly: how it felt to not be her. I asked her to come with me when I got rid of it, and she was surprised but nodded.

"I'm asking you," I said, "because I can't really tell them. I was thinking, though, that maybe you know what it feels like to almost be a mother."

I let the door close as she sat there on her purple comforter, looking not sure whether to feel insulted or understood.

I wanted to schedule it in Brooklyn, on the off chance that someone I knew would be at the Planned Parenthood in Manhattan, but
Brooklyn was all booked up and they sent me downtown. The whole
place was pink pink pink: shell-pink carpeting, puke-pink plastic
chairs that wobbled if you squirmed, pale pink walls. I signed in
and took a number, imagining I was anyplace else. The DMV, backstage at a beauty pageant, the take-out counter at a restaurant. The
lobby was full of mostly girls, with the occasional boyfriend. A boy
who looked no older than fifteen patted the round belly of his even
younger-looking girlfriend. Another twirled a strand of his girlfriend's hair while she read through a brochure on contraceptives
and occasionally looked up nervously, as though scared someone
would see her there. A grown man squeezed the hand of the young
woman next to him, who looked panicked and terrified.

Laura looked panicked and terrified, too, mesmerized by the tacky
not-quite-tragedy of the waiting room. I imagined (this is what we
did with Laura then: we never asked, we imagined) the doctor's office
she'd visited to be screened and tested and have her eggs removed.
I imagined it blue, with soft music in the background and fresh flowers on the waiting-room table, next to the *New Yorker*. I imagined
people smiled more and struck up conversation easily. The girls there
to donate would feel kinship with Laura, and if the women there
to receive were inclined to be jealous of her youth and beauty and
fertility, their jealousy would recede once they realized they could
afford to buy her.

I wondered if Laura was uncomfortable there. Her childhood

was probably free clinics like the one we were sitting in. The shyness of her voice, the way she sometimes slipped up and had to fix a grammatical error—these hinted that maybe she was what my father would have called white trash if my mother weren't there to say it was a term analogous to *nigger* and he ought to apologize for using it. Impostor or not, she could hide her inadequacy behind salon-lightened hair and a thousand-dollar leather coat. Sitting next to her, I did not feel analogous. They paid her for her potential babies, and they were about to vacuum mine out of me. I felt queasy. I hoped they would forget to call my number. I didn't want or not want the baby, I didn't have any grand political problem with abortion, I didn't have any religion to speak of and thought that if God existed and expected me to follow any particular rules, I was probably going to hell anyway, and not for this. I just didn't want to be there, didn't want to deal with it, didn't want to be any emptier than I already felt. I wanted to be full. That was one of the things the girls in Laura's egg-donor group complained about: the painful part of the drugs they had to take. They felt "full" in their abdomens, swollen with potential for life. I had wanted that forever and had never felt it yet.

"I don't want to do this," I said.

"Me neither," she said, which didn't make a lot of sense, but I didn't really care what she was trying to say right then. I looked at her for a second. Her fingertips were pressed into her temples, and I could see her nails, the French polish on them chipping slightly, and her roots, a few shades darker than the blond of the rest of her hair. Logic was never going to save us, but I started talking anyway.

"If I took summer classes, I could graduate in August. Before the baby. I have good grades, I could get an OK job."

Not a spy. You couldn't spy with a baby. It would cry and blow your cover.

Laura looked the other way.

"I've done this before," she said.

"*This?*" I asked.

"The waiting-room thing. With my older sister, when we were in high school. Twice. She wasn't one of those people who got emotional about it, she just needed me for the ride home."

"What was it like?" I asked.

"The doctors were sweeter to her than I was," Laura said. "I was sitting there waiting for her, and I kept thinking everyone in that room knew someone who knew someone who knew me, and they were all thinking it would be me next, and I'd show them, it never would be."

"It's not you," I said. I looked down at my scuffed red and black Pumas. I thought about kicking her, for reminding me where we came from, for reminding me that I used to think of her as one of us.

"Isn't it?" she asked.

"It's me. You might as well not even be here."

"Then why'd you ask me?"

"Why'd you come?"

"What am I supposed to say?"

"I don't know. What am I supposed to do with a baby?"

"Love it," she said. Her voice sounded like it was about to break.

Love it. Like it was that simple. Like loving something ever paid anyone's rent. I tugged so hard on the strand of hair I'd been twirling that it snapped off. Love it, I thought. Let it be mine. I took a breath.

"I'd need money, though."

I ran through the numbers again. I thought of my baby like a doll, like one in a row of dozens and dozens of fancy toy dolls, all with price tags announcing that I couldn't have them. The money was such an obvious problem that I didn't even get to thinking about any of the others most of the time. It seemed wrong to me, that money should be the difference between a baby and not-a-baby. I had a thing inside of me that I could not afford, and Laura had things inside of her that she couldn't afford not to sell, and on the other end of it there were women spending tens of thousands of dollars to buy them because they felt their own bodies had betrayed them. Any way you looked at it, where there should have been a child, there was a math problem.

"At Financial Aid they'd probably cover my tuition for the summer," I said. "But I'd need the security for an apartment, and something to live on till I could get a job. Plus money for doctors and stuff. Once I graduate I can't get school insurance anymore."

Laura turned and looked at me, and it was not exactly friendship on her face. More like resignation.

"I just got paid," she said softly. "Take it."

I didn't care right then why she was doing it: guilt, or anger, or privilege. I didn't care if she needed it or not. I didn't even have the pride to reject the first offer and make her insist. It wasn't that I'd planned it that way, and I don't know when I knew what I was doing but all of a sudden it was done and I wasn't about to feel guilty.

"All right," I said. "If you can afford that."

She pulled out her checkbook, like it was nothing. I thought of telling her to stop, watched her loopy cursive fill the space of the check. I wondered what I'd say to Rafael, what I'd do when the money ran out, what Laura and I would say to each other for the last few months of what was suddenly my last semester of college. I thought of telling her to stop, but like I was afraid of undoing the knot of cells growing into something alive inside of me, I was afraid of undoing what was happening.

When she handed me the check, I folded it into my wallet and didn't say a word. I didn't think I deserved it, not really, nor did I think she owed me. I thought the universe was a whole series of unfulfilled transactions, checks waiting to be cashed, opportunities waiting to be cashed in, even if they were opportunities made of your own flesh. I thought it was a horrible world to bring a child into, but an even worse world in which to stay a child. I left my number lying on the seat and stood up and walked out to Broadway, Laura behind me. I watched my feet as though they belonged to someone else. I looked up at the sky, feeling grown and full of something sad and aching to be known.

Someone Ought to Tell Her
There's Nowhere to Go

Georgie knew before he left that Lanae would be fucking Kenny by the time he got back to Virginia. At least she'd been up front about it, not like all those other husbands and wives and girlfriends and boyfriends, shined up and cheesing for the five-o'clock news on the day their lovers shipped out and then jumping into bed with each other before the plane landed. When he'd told Lanae about his orders, she'd just lifted an eyebrow, shook her head, and said, "I told you not to join the goddamn army." Before he left for basic training, she'd stopped seeing him, stopped taking his calls, even, said, "I'm not waiting for you to come home dead, and I'm damn sure not having Esther upset when you get killed."

That was how he knew she loved him at least a little bit; she'd brought the kid into it. Lanae wasn't like some single mothers, always throwing their kid up in people's faces. She was fiercely protective of Esther, kept her apart from everything, even him, and they'd been in each other's life so long that he didn't believe for a second that she was really through with him this time. Still, he missed her when everyone else was getting loved visibly and he was standing there with no one to say good-bye to. Even her love was strategic, goddamn her, and he felt more violently toward the men he imagined touching her in his absence than toward the imaginary enemy they'd been war-gaming against. On the plane he had stared out of the window at more water than he'd ever seen at once, and thought of the look on her face when he said good-bye.

She had come to his going-away party like it was nothing, showed up in skintight jeans and that cheap but sweet-smelling baby powder perfume and spent a good twenty minutes exchanging pleasantries with his mother before she even said hello to him. She'd brought a cake that she'd picked up from the bakery at the second restaurant she worked at, told one of the church ladies she was thinking of starting her own cake business. *Really?* Georgie thought, before she winked at him and put a silver fingernail to her lips. Lanae could cook a little, but the only time he remembered her trying to bake she'd burnt a cake she'd made from boxed mix and then tried to cover it up with pink frosting. Esther wouldn't touch the thing, and he'd run out and gotten a Minnie Mouse ice cream cake from the grocery store. He'd found himself silently listing these nonsecrets, the things about Lanae he was certain of: she couldn't bake, there was a thin but awful scar running down the back of her right calf, her eyes were amber in the right light.

They'd grown up down the street from each other. He could not remember a time before they were friends, but she'd had enough time to get married and divorced and produce a little girl before he thought to kiss her for the first time, only a few months before he got his orders. In fairness, she was not exactly beautiful; it had taken some time for him to see past that. Her face was pleasant but plain, her features so simple that if she were a cartoon she'd seem deliberately underdrawn. She was not big, exactly, but pillowy, like if you pressed your hand into her it would keep sinking and sinking because there was nothing solid to her. It bothered him to think of Kenny putting his hand on her that way, Kenny who'd once assigned numbers to all the waitresses at Ruby Tuesday based on the quality of their asses, Kenny who'd probably never be gentle enough to notice what her body did while it was his.

It wasn't Lanae who met him at the airport when he landed back where he'd started. It was his mother, looking small in the crowd of people waiting for arrivals. Some of them were bored, leaning up against the wall like they were in line for a restaurant table; others peered around the gate like paparazzi waiting for the right shot to happen. His mother was up in front, squinting at him like she wasn't sure he was real. She was in her nurse's uniform, and it made her look a little ominous. When he came through security she ran up to hug him so he couldn't breathe. "Baby," she said, then asked how the connecting flight had been, and then talked about everything but what mattered. Perhaps after all of his letters home she was used to unanswered questions, because she didn't ask any, not about the war, not about his health, not about the conditions of his honorable discharge or what he intended to do upon his return to civilian society.

She was all weather and light gossip through the parking lot. "The cherry blossoms are beautiful this year," she was saying as they rode down the Dulles Toll Road, and if it had been Lanae saying something like that he would have said *Cherry blossoms? Are you fucking kidding me?* but because it was his mother things kept up like that all the way around 495 and back to Alexandria. It was still too early in the morning for real rush-hour traffic, and they made it in twenty minutes. The house was as he'd remembered it: old, the bright robin's egg blue of the paint cheerful in a painfully false way, like a woman wearing red lipstick and layers of foundation caked over wrinkles. Inside, the surfaces were all coated with a thin layer of dust, and it made him feel guilty his mother had to do all of this housework herself, even though when he was home he'd almost never cleaned anything.

He'd barely put his bags down when she was off to work, still not able to take the whole day off. She left with promises of dinner later. In her absence it struck him that it had been a long time since he'd heard silence. In the desert there was always noise. When it was not the radio, or people talking, or shouting, or shouting at him, it was the dull purr of machinery providing a constant background soundtrack, or the rhythmic pulse of sniper fire. Now it was a weekday in the suburbs and the lack of human presence made him anxious. He turned the TV on and off four times, flipping through talk shows and soap operas and thinking this was something like what had happened to him: someone had changed the channel on his life. The abruptness of the transition overrode the need for social protocol, so without calling first he got into the old Buick and drove to Lanae's, the feel of the leather steering wheel strange beneath his hands. The brakes screeched every time he stepped on them, and he realized he should have asked his mother how the car was running before taking it anywhere, but the problem seemed appropriate: he had started this motion, and the best thing to do was not to stop it.

Kenny's car outside of Lanae's duplex did not surprise him, nor did it deter him. He parked in one of the visitor spaces and walked up to ring the bell.

"Son of a bitch! What's good?" Kenny asked when he answered the door, as if Georgie had been gone for a year on a beer run.

"I'm back," he said, unnecessarily. "How you been, man?"

Kenny looked like he'd been Kenny. He'd always been a big guy, but he was getting soft around the middle. His hair was freshly cut in a fade, and he was already in uniform, wearing a shiny gold name tag that said KENNETH, and beneath that, MANAGER, which had not been true when Georgie left. Georgie could smell the apartment through the door, Lanae's perfume and floral air freshener not masking that something had been cooked with grease that morning.

"Not, bad," he said. "I've been holding it down over here while you been holding it down over there. Glad you came back in one piece."

Kenny gave him a one-armed hug, and for a minute Georgie felt like an asshole for wanting to say, *Holding it down? You've been serving people KFC.*

"Look, man, I was on my way to work, but we'll catch up later, all right?" Kenny said, moving out of the doorway to reveal Lanae standing there, still in the T-shirt she'd slept in. Her hair was pulled back in a head scarf, and it made her eyes look huge. Kenny was out the door with a nod and a shoulder clasp, not so much as a backward glance at Lanae standing there. The casual way he left them alone together bothered Georgie. He wasn't sure if Kenny didn't consider him a threat or simply didn't care what Lanae did; either way he was annoyed.

"Hey," said Lanae, her voice soft, and he realized he hadn't thought this visit through any further than that.

"Hi," he said, and looked at the clock on the wall, which was an hour behind schedule. He thought to mention this, then thought against it.

"Georgie!" Esther yelled through the silence, running out of the kitchen, her face sticky with pancake syrup. He was relieved she remembered his name. Her hair was done in pigtails with little pink barrettes on them; they matched her socks and skirt. Lanae could win a prize for coordinating things.

"Look at you, little ma," he said, scooping her up and kissing her cheek. "Look how big you got."

"Look how bad she got, you mean," Lanae said. "Tell Georgie how you got kicked out of day care."

"I got kicked out of day care," Esther said matter-of-factly. Georgie tried not to laugh. Lanae rolled her eyes.

"She hides too much," she said. "Every time they take the kids somewhere, this one hides, and they gotta hold everyone up looking for her. Last time they found her, she scratched the teacher who tried to get her back on the bus. She can't pull this kind of stuff when she starts kindergarten."

Lanae sighed, and reached up to put her fingers in her hair, but all it did was push the scarf back. Take it off, he wanted to say. Take it off, and put clothes on. He wanted it to feel like real life again, like their life again, and with him dressed and wearing cologne for the first time in months, and her standing there in a scarf and T-shirt, all shiny Vaselined thighs and gold toenails, they looked mismatched.

"Look, have some breakfast if you want it," she said. "I'll be out in a second. I need to take a shower, and then I gotta work on finding this one a babysitter before my shift starts."

"When does it start?"

"Two."

"I can watch her. I'm free."

Lanae gave him an appraising look. "What *are* you doing these days?"

"Today, nothing."

"Tomorrow?"

"Don't know yet."

"I talked to your mom a little while ago," Lanae said, which was her way of telling him she knew. Of course she knew. How could Lanae not know, gossipy mother or no gossipy mother?

"I'm fine," he said. "I'll take good care of her."

"If Dee doesn't get back to me, you might have to," said Lanae. She walked off and Georgie made himself at home in her kitchen, grabbing a plate from the dish rack and taking the last of the eggs and bacon from the pans on the stove. Esther sat beside him and colored as he poured syrup over his breakfast.

"So, what do you keep hiding from?" he asked.

"Nothing." Esther shrugged. "I just like the trip places better. Day care smells funny and the kids are dumb."

"What did I tell you about stupid people?" Georgie asked.

"I forget." Esther squinted. "You were gone a long time."

"Well, I'm back now, and you're not going to let stupid people bother you anymore," Georgie said, even though neither of these promises was his to make.

Honestly, watching Esther was good for him. His mother was perplexed, Kenny was amused, Lanae was skeptical. But Esther could not go back to her old day care, and Dee, the woman down the street who ran an unlicensed day care in her living room, plopped the kids in front of the downstairs television all afternoon, and could only be torn away from her soaps upstairs if one of them hit someone or broke something. It wasn't hard for Georgie to be the best alternative. He became adequate as a caretaker. He took Esther on trips. They read and reread her favorite books. He learned to cut the crusts off of peanut butter and jelly sandwiches. Over and above her protests that the old sitter had let the kids stay up to watch late-night comedy, he made sure she was washed and in bed and wearing matching pajamas by the time Lanae and Kenny got home from their evening shifts.

"Are you sure it doesn't remind you . . ." his mother started once, after gently suggesting he look for a real job, but she let the thought trail off unfinished.

"I wasn't *babysitting* over there, Ma."

"I know," she said, but she didn't, or she wouldn't have thought to put Esther and those other kids in the same sentence.

The truth was Esther was the opposite of a reminder. In his old life, his job had been to knock on strangers' doors in the middle of the night, hold them at gunpoint, and convince them to trust him. That was the easiest part of it. They went at night because during daytime the snipers had a clear shot at them and anyone who opened the door, but even in the dark, a bullet or an IED could take you out like that. Sometimes when they got to a house there were already bodies. Other times there was nothing: a thin film of dust over whatever was left, things too heavy for the family to carry and too worthless for anyone to steal.

The sisters were sitting in the dark, huddled on the floor with their parents, when Georgie's unit pushed through the door. Pretty girls, big black eyes and sleepy baby-doll faces. The little one cried when they first came through the door, and the older one, maybe nine, clamped her hand tightly over the younger girl's mouth, like they'd been ordered not to make any noise. The father was soft-spoken—angry but reasonable. Usually, Georgie stood back and kept an eye out for trouble, let the lieutenant do the talking, but this time he went over to the girls himself, reached out his hand and shook their tiny ones, moist with heat and fear. He handed them each a piece of the candy they were supposed to give to children in cooperative families, and stepped back awkwardly. The older one smiled back at him, her missing two front teeth somehow reminding him of home.

They were not, in the grand scheme of things, anyone special. There were kids dying all over the place. Still, when they went back the next day, to see if the father would answer some more questions about his neighbors, and the girls were lying there, throats slit, bullets to the head, blood everywhere but parents nowhere to be found, he stepped outside of the house to vomit.

When Georgie was twelve, a station wagon skidded on the ice and swerved into his father's Tercel, crushing the car and half of his father, who bled into an irreversible coma before Georgie and his mother got to the hospital to see him. Because his mother had to be sedated at the news, he'd stood at his father's bedside alone, staring at the body, the way the part beneath the sheet was unnaturally crumpled, the way his face began to look like melted wax, the way his lips remained slightly parted.

Georgie hadn't known, at first, that the sisters would stick with him like that.

"What's fucked up," Georgie said to Jones two days after, "is that I wished for a minute it was our guys who did it, some psycho who lost it. The way that kid looked at me, like she really thought I came to save her. I don't want to think about them coming for her family because we made them talk. I don't want to be the reason they did her like that."

"What's the difference between you and some other asshole?" Jones said. "Either nobody's responsible for nothing, or every last motherfucker on this planet is going to hell someday."

After that, he'd turn around in the shower, the girls would be there. He'd be sleeping, and he'd open his eyes to see the little one hiding in the corner of his room. He was jumpy and too spooked to sleep. He told Ramirez about it, and Ramirez said you didn't get to pick your ghosts, your ghosts picked you.

"Still," he said. "Lieutenant sends you to talk to someone, don't say that shit. White people don't believe in ghosts."

But he told the doctors everything, and then some. He didn't care anymore what his file said, as long as it got him the fuck out of that place. And the truth is, right before the army let him go, sent him packing with a prescription and a once-a-month check-in with the shrink at the VA hospital, it had gotten really bad. One night he was sure the older girl had come to him in a dream and told him Peterson had come back and killed her, skinny Peterson who didn't even like to kill the beetles that slipped into their blankets every night, but nonetheless he'd held Peterson at gunpoint until Ramirez came in and snapped him out of it. Another time, he got convinced Jones really was going to kill him one day, and ran up to him outside of mess hall, grabbing for his pistol; three or four guys had to pull him off. Once, in the daytime, he thought he saw one of the dead girls, bold as brass, standing outside on the street they were patrolling. He went to shake her by the shoulders, ask her what she'd been playing at, pretending to be dead all this time, but he'd only just grabbed her when Ramirez pulled him off of her, shaking his head, and when he looked back at the girl's tear-streaked face before she ran for it like there was no tomorrow, he realized she was someone else entirely. Ramirez put an arm around him and started to say something, then seemed to think better of it. He looked down the road at the place that girl had just been.

"The fuck you think she's running to so fast, anyway? Someone ought to tell her there's nowhere to go."

Sometimes Esther called him *Daddy*. When it started out, it seemed harmless enough. They were always going places that encouraged fantasy. Chuck E. Cheese's, where the giant rat sang and served pizza. The movies, where princesses lived happily ever after. The zoo, where animals that could have killed you in their natural state looked bored and docile behind high fences. Glitter Girl, Esther's favorite store in the mall, where girls three and up could get manicures, and any girl of any age could buy a crown or a pink T-shirt that said ROCK STAR. What was a pretend family relationship, compared to all that? Besides, it made people less nervous. When she'd introduced him to strangers as her babysitter, all six feet and two hundred and five pounds of him, they'd raised their eyebrows and looked at him as though he might be some kind of predator. Now people thought it was sweet when they went places together.

"This is my daddy," Esther told the manicurist at Glitter Girl, where Georgie had just let Esther get her nails painted fuchsia. She smiled at him conspiratorially. He had reminded her, gently, that Mommy might not understand about their make-believe family, and they should keep it to themselves for now.

"Day off, huh?" said the manicurist. She looked like a college kid, a cute redhead with dangly pom-pom earrings. Judging by the pocketbook she'd draped over the chair beside her, she was working there for kicks: if the logo on the bag was real, it was worth three of Georgie's old army paychecks.

"I'm on leave," he said. "Army. I was in Iraq for a year. Just trying to spend as much time with her as I can before I head back." He sat up straighter, afraid somehow she'd see through the lie and refuse to believe he'd been a soldier at all. When they'd walked in, she'd looked at him with polite skepticism, as if in one glance she could tell that Esther's coordinated clothes came from Target, that he was out of real work and his gold watch was a knockoff that sometimes turned his wrist green, like perhaps the pity in her smile would show them they were in the wrong store, without the humiliation of price tags.

"Wow," she murmured now, almost deferentially. She looked up and swept an arc of red hair away from her face so she could look at him directly. "A year in Iraq. I can't imagine. Of course you'll spend all the time you can with her. They grow up so fast." She shook her head with a sincerity he found oddly charming in a woman who worked in a store that sold halter tops for girls with no breasts.

"Tell you what, sweetheart," she said to Esther. "Since your daddy's such a brave man, and you're such a good girl for letting him go off and protect us, I'm going to do a little something extra for you. Do you want some nail gems?"

Esther nodded, and Georgie turned his head away so the manicurist wouldn't see him smirk. Nail gems. Cherry blossoms. The things people offered him by way of consolation.

· · ·

When Esther's nails were drying, tiny heart-shaped rhinestones in the center of each one, and the salesgirl had gone to wait on the next customer, a miniature blonde with a functional razor phone but no parent in sight, Esther turned to him accusingly.

"You're going away," she said.

"I'm not," he said.

"You told the lady you were."

"It was pretend," he said, closing his eyes. "This is a make-believe place, it's OK to pretend here. Just like I'm your pretend Daddy."

He realized he had bought her silence on one lie by offering her another, but he couldn't see any way out of it. So they wouldn't tell Lanae. So the salesgirl would flirt with him a little and do a little something extra for Esther next time. He *had* made sacrifices. Esther deserved nice things. Her mother worked two jobs and her real father was somewhere in Texas with his second wife. So what if it was the wrong things they were being rewarded for?

At the counter, he pulled out his wallet and paid for Esther's manicure with the only card that wasn't maxed out. Esther ignored the transaction entirely, wandering to the other end of the counter and reappearing with a purple flier. It had a holographic background and under the fluorescent mall light seemed, appropriately, to glitter.

Come see Mindy with Glitter Girl! exclaimed the flier. Mindy was a tiny brunette, nine, maybe, who popped a gum bubble and held one hand on her hip, the other extended to show off her nails, purple with gold stars in the middle.

"Everybody wants to see Mindy," said the manicurist. She winked at them, then ducked down to file his receipt.

"Maybe we could go," he said, reaching for the flier Esther was holding, but the smile that started for her dimples faded just as quickly.

"I don't really wanna," she said. "It's prolly dumb anyway."

He followed her eyes to the ticket price and understood that she'd taken in the number of zeros. He was stung for a minute that even a barely five-year-old was that acutely aware of his limitations, then charmed by her willingness to protect him from them. It shouldn't be like that, he thought; a kid shouldn't understand that there's anything her parents can't do. Then again, he was not her father. He was a babysitter. He had less than a quarter of the price of a ticket in his personal bank account—what was left of his disability check after he helped his mother out with the rent and utilities. He spent most of what Lanae paid him to watch Esther on Esther herself, because it made Lanae feel good to pay him, and him feel good not to take her money. He folded the Mindy flier into his pocket, and gently pulled off the twenty-dollar glittered tiara Esther had perched on her head to leave it on the counter. "Mommy will come back and get it later," he lied, over and above her objections. Even the way he disappointed her came as a relief.

Of course, the thought had crossed his mind. He never thought Kenny and Lanae were the real thing—didn't even think they did, really. Things had changed between her and Kenny in the year Georgie had been gone—softened and become more comfortable than whatever casual on-again, off-again thing they had before she and Georgie had dated—but he wasn't inclined to believe it was real. He pictured himself and Lanae as statues on a wedding cake: they were a pair. Kenny was a pastime. How could Georgie not hope that when she saw the way he was with Esther, she'd see the rest of it sooner?

But it wasn't like that was the *reason* he liked watching her. Not the only reason. Esther was a good kid. He thought it meant something, the way she didn't act up with him, didn't fuss and hide the way she'd used to at day care. But yeah, he got to talk to Lanae some. At night, when Lanae came home, and Esther was in bed, and Kenny was still at work for an hour, because being manager meant he was the last to leave the KFC, they talked a little. Usually he turned on a TV show right before she came in, so he could pretend he was watching it, but mostly he didn't need the excuse to stay. It was Lanae who sat with him that week after his father had died, Lanae who, when she found out she was pregnant with Esther, had called him, not her husband or her best girlfriend. There was an easy kind of comfort between them, and when she came home and sat beside him on the couch and kicked off her flats and began to rub her own tired feet with mint-scented lotion, it was only his fear of upsetting something that kept him from reaching out to do it for her.

When Lanae came home the day he'd taken Esther to the mall, he wanted to tell her about the girl, the way she'd smiled at him, and scan her face for a flicker of jealousy. Then he remembered he'd earned the smile by lying. So instead he unfolded the Mindy flier from his pocket and passed it to her.

"Can you believe this shit?" he asked. "Five hundred dollars a pop for a kids' show? When we were kids, we were happy if we got five dollars for the movies and a dollar for some candy to sneak in."

"Hey." Lanae grinned. "I wanted two dollars, for candy *and* a soda. You were cheap." She held the flier at arm's length, then turned it sideways, like Mindy would make more sense that way.

"Esther wants to go to this?"

"The lady at Glitter Girl said all the girls do. She said in most cities the tickets already sold out."

"That whole store is creepy, anyway. And even if it was free, Esther don't need to be at a show where some nine-year-old in a belly shirt is singing at people to *Come pop my bubble*. Fucking perverts," Lanae said.

"Who's a pervert?" asked Kenny. Georgie hadn't heard him come in, but Lanae didn't look surprised to see him standing in the doorway. He was carrying a steaming, grease-spotted bag that was meant to be dinner, which was usually Georgie's cue to leave. As Kenny walked toward them, Georgie slid away from Lanae on the couch, not because they'd been especially close to begin with, but because he wanted to maintain the illusion that they might have been. But Lanae stood up anyway, to kiss Kenny on the cheek as she handed him the flier.

"These people," said Lanae, "are perverts."

Kenny shook his head at the flier. Georgie silently reminded himself of the sophomore Kenny had dated their senior year of high school, a girl not much bigger than Mindy, and how Kenny used to joke about how easy it was to pick her up and throw her around the room during sex.

"Esther ain't going to this shit," Kenny said. "This is nonsense."

"She can't," said Georgie. "You can't afford it."

Kenny stepped toward him, then back again just as quickly.

"Fuck you, man," said Kenny. "Fuck you and the two dollars an hour we pay you."

He pounded a fist at the wall beside him, and then walked toward the hallway. A second later Georgie heard the bedroom door slam.

"Georgie," said Lanae, already walking after Kenny, "you don't have to be an asshole. He's not the way you remember him. He's trying. You need to try harder. And this Mindy shit? Esther will forget about it. Kids don't know. Next week she'll be just as worked up about wanting fifty cents for bubble gum."

But Esther couldn't have forgotten about it. Mindy was on the side of the bus they took to the zoo. Mindy was on the nightly news, and every other commercial between kids' TV shows. Mindy was on the radio, lisping, *Pop my bub-ble, pop pop my bub-ble.* What he felt for Mindy was barely short of violence. He restrained himself from shouting back at the posters, and the radio, and the television: *Mindy, what is your position on civilians in combat zones? Mindy, what's your position on waterboarding? Mindy, do you think Iraq was a mistake?* He got letters, occasionally, from people who were still there: one from

Jones, one from Ramirez, three from guys he didn't know that well and figured must have been lonely enough that they'd write to anyone. He hadn't read them.

He went back to the mall alone on the Saturday after he'd pissed Kenny off. He told himself he was there to talk to the manicure girl, pick up a little present for Esther, and meanwhile maybe get something going on in his life besides wet dreams about Lanae, who'd been curt with him ever since the thing he said to Kenny. But when he got to the store, the redhead was leaning across the counter, giving a closed-mouth kiss on the lips to a kid in a UVA sweatshirt. He looked like an advertisement for fraternities. Georgie started to walk out, convinced he'd been wrong about the whole plan, but when the boyfriend turned around and walked away from the counter, the redhead saw him and waved.

"Hey!" she called. "Where's your little girl?"

"I came to pick up something to surprise her," he said. "She's been asking for a princess dress to go with the crown her mom got her."

He was pleased with the lie, until the redhead, whose name tag read ANNIE, led him over to the dress section and he realized he'd worn suits to weddings that cost less.

"Come to think of it," he said, "I'm not sure of her size. Maybe I oughta come back with her mother. Meantime, maybe she would like a wand."

"That's a good idea," said Annie. "All the kids are into magic these days."

Annie grabbed the wand that matched the crown and led him

back to the register. The Mindy fliers had been replaced by a counter-length overhead banner. Mindy's head sat suspended on a background of pink bubbles.

"What's this Mindy kid do, anyway?" he asked.

"She sings."

"She sing well?"

"It's just cute, mostly. She has her own TV show, and her older sister sings, too, but sexier. You get tickets for your daughter?"

"Nah," he said. "Bit pricey for a five-year-old. Maybe next year."

"They ought to pay you people more. It's a shame. It's important, what you do."

She said this like someone who had read it somewhere. It would have seemed stupid to disagree and pathetic to nod, so he stood there, waiting for his change.

"Hey," said Annie. "We're having this contest to win tickets to the show. Limo ride, dinner, backstage passes, the whole shebang. All you have to do is make a video of your daughter saying why she wants to go. I bet if your daughter talks about how good she was while you were gone, she'd have a shot. It's right here, the contest info," she said, picking up a flier and circling the website. "Doesn't have to be anything fancy—you could do it on a camera phone."

"Thanks," he said, reaching to take the bag from her.

"Really," she said. "I mean it. Who's got a better story than you? Deadline's Tuesday. It'd be nice if they gave it to someone who deserved it."

• • •

He liked to think that Annie's encouragement was tacit consent. He liked to think that if he'd had longer to think about it, he would have realized it was a bad idea. But as it was, by Sunday he'd convinced himself that it was a good idea, and by Monday he'd convinced Esther, who, after hearing the word "limousine," needed only the slightest convincing that this was not the *bad* kind of lie. And when she started the first time, it wasn't even a lie, really. *Hi Glitter Girl,* she began, all on her own, *for a whole year while he was in Iraq, I missed my Daddy.* OK, so he wasn't her father, but he liked to think she *had* missed him that much. When she said how much she wanted for him to take her to the show now that he was back, he thought it was honest: she wanted not just to see the show but to see it with him. He had downloaded the video from his phone and played it back for her, and was ready to send it like that, when Esther decided it wasn't good enough.

"Let's tell how you saved people," she said. "We have more time left."

He hesitated, but before he could say no, she asked him to tell her who he'd saved, and looking at her—the hopeful glimmer in her eyes, her pigtails tied with elastics with red beads on the end, matching her jumpsuit and the ruffles on her socks—he realized her intentions had been more sincere than his. How could they not be? Esther didn't doubt for a second that he had a heroic story to tell. He closed his eyes.

"Two girls," he said, finally. "A girl about Mindy's age. She was missing her two front teeth. And her little sister, who she loved a lot. Some bad men wanted to hurt them, and I scared off the bad men and helped them get away."

"Where'd they go then?"

"Back to their families," he said. He opened his mouth to say something, but nothing came out.

"Start the movie over," Esther said. "I'm going to say that too."

Somehow, he was not expecting the cameras. It was such a small thing, he'd thought. But there was Esther's video, labeled CONTEST WINNER! ESTHER, AGE 5, ALEXANDRIA, VA, right on the Glitter Girl website. It was only a small relief that this was the last place Lanae would ever go herself, but who knew who else might stumble upon it? He'd named himself as her parent, given his name and phone and authorized the use of the images, and now he had messages, not just from Glitter Girl, who'd called to get their particulars, but from *The Washington Post*, and Channel 4 and Channel 7 news. Even after the first few, he thought he could get this back in the bottle, that Lanae would never need to know. In his bathroom mirror, in the morning, he practiced what to say to the journalists to make them go away. He tried to think of ways to answer questions without making them think to ask more.

Listen, he told the Channel 4 reporter, I'd love to do a story, but Esther's mother has this crazy ex-boyfriend who's been threatening her for years, and if Esther's last name or picture is in the paper, we could be in a lot of trouble. Look, he told the Channel 7 reporter, the kid's been through hell this year, with me gone and her mom barely holding it together. It was hard enough for her to say it once. Please contact Glitter Girl for official publicity.

It was the *Post* reporter that did them in, the *Post* reporter and the free makeover Esther was supposed to get on her official prize pickup day. He figured it was back-page news, and anyway, Esther was so excited about it. They would paint her nails and take some pictures and give them the tickets, and that would be the end of it. When they walked into the store a week later, there was a giant pink welcome banner that proclaimed CONGRATULATIONS ESTHER! and clouds of pale pink and white balloons. All of the employees and invited local media clapped their hands. Annie was there, beaming at them when they walked in, like she'd just won a prize for her science fair project. The CEO of Glitter Girl, a severe-looking woman with incongruous big blond hair, hugged Esther and shook his hand. Mindy's music played on repeat over the loudspeakers.

There was cake and sparkling cider. The CEO gave a heartfelt toast. Annie gave him a hug and slipped her phone number into his pocket. One of the other employees led Esther off. She came back in a sequined pink dress, a long brown wig, fluttery fake eyelashes, pink lipstick, and shiny purple nails. People took pictures. He was alarmed at first, but she turned to him and smiled like he'd never seen a kid smile before, and he thought it couldn't be so bad, to give someone exactly what she wanted. Finally, the CEO of Glitter Girl handed them the tickets. She said Esther had already received some fan mail and handed him a pile of letters. He looked at the return addresses: California, Florida, New York, Canada.

"Is there anything you'd like to say to all your fans, Esther?" shouted one of the reporters.

"I want to say," said Esther, "I am so happy to win this, but mostly I am so happy to have my daddy."

She turned and winked at him. She smiled a movie-star grin. There was lipstick on her teeth. For the first time, he realized how badly he'd fucked up.

It was two days later the first story ran. Esther had told the *Post* reporter her mommy worked at the Ruby Tuesday on Route 7, but when the reporter called her there to get a quote, Lanae had no idea what she was talking about, said she did have a daughter named Esther, but her daughter's father was in Texas and had never been in the army, and her daughter wasn't allowed in Glitter Girl or at any Mindy concert.

She called Georgie on her break to ask him about it, but he said it must have been a mix-up, he didn't know anything about it.

"You'd damn well better not be lying to me, Georgie," she said, which meant she already knew he was.

That night he called the number Annie had given to him, wondered if she could meet him somewhere, pictured her long legs wrapped around his.

"Look," she said softly, "I'm sorry. I was being impulsive the other day. You're married, and I'm engaged, and I'm really proud of you, but it's just better if everything stays aboveboard. Let's not hurt anyone we don't have to."

Georgie hung up. He went downstairs and watched television with his mother, until she turned it off and looked at him.

"You know I watch the news during my break at the hospital," she said.

"Uh-huh," said Georgie. "They're not still shortchanging you on your break time, are they?"

"Don't change the subject. Other day I coulda swore I saw Esther on TV. Channel 9. All dressed up like some hoochie princess, and talking about her *daddy*, who was in the *army*."

"Small world," said Georgie. "A lot of coincidences."

But it was a lie, about the world being small. It was big enough. By the time he drove to Lanae's house the next morning, there was a small crowd of reporters outside. They didn't even notice him pull up. Kenny kept opening the door, telling them they had the wrong house. Finally, he had to go to work, walked out in his uniform. Flashbulbs snapped.

"Are you the one who encouraged the child to lie, or does the mother have another boyfriend?" yelled one reporter.

Georgie couldn't hear what Kenny said back, but for the first time in his life, Georgie thought Kenny looked brave.

"Did you do this for the money?" yelled another. "Was this the child's idea?"

All day, it was like that. Long after Kenny had left, the reporters hung out on the front steps, broadcasting to each other. Lanae had already given back the tickets; beyond that, she had given no comment. He could imagine the face she made when she refused to comment, the steely eyes, the way everything about her could freeze.

"How," the reporters wanted to know, "did this happen?"

Their smugness made him angry. There were so many things they could never understand about how, so many explanations they've never bothered to demand. How could it *not* have happened?

At night, when no one had opened the door for hours, the reporters trickled off one by one, their questions still unanswered. Lanae must have taken the day off from work: her car was still in its parking space, the lights in the house still on. Finally, he made his way to the house and rang the doorbell. She was at the peephole in an instant. She left the chain on and opened the door as wide as it could go without releasing it.

"Georgie," she said. She shook her head, then leaned her forehead against the edge of the door so that just her eyeball was looking at his. "Georgie, go away."

"Lanae," he said. "You know I didn't mean it to go like this."

"Georgie, my five-year-old's been crying all day. My phone number, here and at my job, is on the Internet. People from Iowa to goddamn Denmark have been calling my house all day, calling my baby a liar and a little bitch. She's confused. You're confused. I think you need to go for a while."

"Where?" he asked.

He waited there on the front step until she'd turned her head from his, stepped back into the house, and squeezed the door shut. He kept standing there, long after the porch light went off, not so much making an argument as waiting for an answer.

The King of a Vast Empire

Two weeks before Thanksgiving, my sister called to tell me she'd decided to be an elephant trainer. At first, the only thing I could think of elephants being trained for was the circus, which we had never been to as kids, so I pictured cartoon elephants balancing on giant plastic beach balls, like in *Dumbo*. I thought for a second that Liddie was dropping out of school altogether to wear sparkly spandex and chase them around with a baton, which seemed unlikely on any number of counts. My sister liked college, had once been banned from the local Fluff N Stuff pet boutique for trying to liberate a show poodle, and hadn't been near a stage since she quit dance school, in the sixth grade, after calling its photo display of smiling ballerinas *the hall of kiddie porn for voyeurs without the balls to be real pedophiles,* in front of the academy's male director. Liddie was not running off to join the circus. What she actually had in mind was working at some kind of conservatory for elephants with post-traumatic stress syndrome.

"Elephants experience trauma the way humans do," she informed me. "They're fascinating animals."

"Humans aren't that fascinating," I said.

What was happening with me right then was, the first woman I'd been with for longer than a year had left me, my car had died unexpectedly, and someone named Carlos was stealing my identity and improving my credit in the process. I'd found out the last bit while trying to buy a used car, and had yet to do anything about it because I kind of liked the idea of someone wanting to be me. If I were my parents, I'm not sure Liddie's the kid I'd worry about, but maybe they'd given up on me.

My mother called three days after Liddie had.

"Terrence," she said, "you need to talk to your sister."

"I just talked to my sister," I said.

"Well, talk to her again. She's changed her major to some sort of comparative biology nonsense, and she's not coming home for Thanksgiving this year."

I thought of last year, when Liddie had come home for Thanksgiving with her white anarchist poet boyfriend and caused my mother to glare at me every time Liddie referred to Thanksgiving as the Day of Native Resistance, as if I were somehow responsible for this. I'd played a drinking game that involved taking a shot of whatever was convenient every time a glare happened, and was utterly shitfaced by the time Liddie drove me home and told me that I ought to watch being drunk around our parents on holidays because it obviously upset them, as if she'd been Marcia Brady all night.

I wasn't too broken up about scaling back Thanksgiving this year. Liddie and I did better with each other on our own terms. When I talked to her, she said she wasn't mad or anything, it was just that changing her major from ethnic studies to comparative biology meant switching into a lot of classes late in the semester, and she had some catch-up studying to do. Liddie seemed OK to me, or at least she'd had way more alarming phases. I figured the elephant thing would end, as had the summer she converted to Judaism and the year she stopped eating cooked food.

Difficult phases notwithstanding, Liddie was the most together person in my life, which says maybe more about my life than Liddie's togetherness. I was a mess before I met Gabi, but it got worse when she left me. We'd had something like a fight the week before she took off, but nothing compared to the worst of them. Fighting with Gabi, I'd thought, was like fighting with Liddie: at the end of the day she wasn't going anywhere. Gabi, understand, was addicted to bad news. Every morning she read five newspapers in three languages, and if she couldn't get to a newspaper, she'd start shaking and looking for the nearest television. On really bad days she binged and purged on old microfiche the way bulimic girls I'd known in college did with food, sucking it all in and then hurling it back out into the world at the first opportunity. The worst of the news she thought was appropriate to share in the middle of sex, and when I say worst I mean: dismembered child soldiers, bomb victims burned beyond recognition, elderly women beaten and raped, and when I say middle I mean we're naked and sweaty and I'm inside her and it's really not the time. The last time I stopped and said she was fucking weird and perverted.

Without bothering to put clothes on, she'd proceeded to explain to me, not for the first time, that really, all pleasure was perverse, that it was perverse to ever enjoy anything in such an awful world, that any moment of happiness was selfish when infinite horror was always happening somewhere else.

"Tell me," she'd said. "Tell me, Terrence, how you can ever be happy about something as stupid as sex, in a world where children are beheaded for no reason. Doesn't that make you really fucking sick?"

"You make me really fucking sick sometimes, Gabi," I said.

She silently walked into the kitchen, still naked, opened the cabinet, and proceeded to line up my cherry-red drinking glasses and one by one throw them at the living room wall, waiting for the last to shatter before reaching for the next. When she finished she looked up.

"If you're going to call me crazy, I'm damn well going to act it," she said.

Technically, I hadn't called her crazy. I did not, in fact, think she looked so much like a crazy person as a quite rational and calculating person behaving the way she thought a crazy person might—a prospect I found significantly more frightening and not entirely unattractive. I said nothing, went for a long drive, and returned to find the glass swept up and a new set of glasses lined up on the kitchen counter. I thought it was a peace offering and not a good-bye.

I never paid for the newspapers after she left and most of them stopped coming, but the German paper still came weekly. It was a week behind the present and in a language I didn't speak, but I read it religiously, reveled in its deliberate and drawn-out words. I thought that so long as you didn't understand a thing, it was a god-damn lovely world.

Two months after that I bought the new car, and Jane the credit bureau lady, who somehow managed to give her voice the blank intonation of a dial tone, informed me that my credit report had been red-flagged for an unusual amount of activity and I ought to review it to make sure it was all mine. I didn't; I was vaguely flattered. Plus, I had to consider the minuscule improvement in my credit score. I'd almost forgotten about it by the time the cops showed up a month later. I'd had the day off from the bookstore, and was stretched out in bed in my boxers and a T-shirt when they knocked. I answered the door just like that because even after the breakup, the only person I could think of who'd drop by in the middle of a weekday afternoon without a phone call was Gabi. The sight of two of Fairfax County's finest was a disappointment.

"You Carlos Aguilar?" they asked.

I tried to squint at their badges, wondering whether it was a trick.

"No," I said, after a second.

It was cleared up pretty quickly. I may have been brown, but my Spanish was pathetic, and I had a wallet full of crap with my name on it: license, employee ID, college ID, ID from the university where I'd pretended I was going to get a master's, library card, Giant discount card, Hollywood video card, et cetera. Enough to prove that I never let go of things, and that I was not who they were looking for.

According to the cops, Carlos was in serious trouble. He was facing several counts of credit card fraud for impersonating other people, some of whom now owed thousands of dollars. Carlos had also been selling people's Social Security numbers on the black market. Mine he was using to be a good citizen, getting the cards he paid on time, apparently renting an apartment in my name. The cops left me with a number to call in case I had any more trouble. I thought about Carlos during the next few days, feeling a certain solidarity with him. I knew most likely I'd just been careless with some kind of important paperwork, but I couldn't shake the feeling I'd been chosen for a reason.

Bored and curious, I spent a lunch break doing an Internet search for myself and pulled up six addresses, one of which was my parents' house, one of which was the shithole apartment I'd had in college, and one of which was my present address. The most recent of the other addresses I thought I recognized as an apartment complex just over the Wilson Bridge, in Maryland. I considered going there, maybe to introduce myself, maybe just to watch for a while, to see if I could pick this guy out of a lineup. The possibilities of such a situation seemed limitless, but the fear of having to explain myself put a stop to most of them. I thought about giving the cops the other address I'd found, but I figured they had people who got paid for that. I'd never even bothered to file any of the things they told me to. I had an imaginary conversation with Gabi about it, in which she told me this was the physical manifestation of my existential crisis, and I told her to stop talking bullshit and then left the room.

While I was having imaginary conversations with my ex-girlfriend, Liddie was finishing up her first semester of junior year at Harvard. It was no wonder that even people who'd known me for the three years that she didn't exist often mistook her for the older sibling. I always thought it was because of the accident, the one she swore that she remembered in perfect detail. Driving us back from the city, Dad had slammed into a car stopped in the middle of the highway. I was nine and sleeping and was carried out of the car in perfect health. Liddie, six and wide-awake, was hit by a piece of flying glass and put in the same ambulance as the children in the other car, two of whom died on the way to the hospital. Liddie was released a few hours later with twenty-five stitches across her forehead. They left a faint scar when they came out.

When Liddie was twelve, a plastic surgeon neighbor mentioned to my mother that Liddie's scar could probably be surgically corrected.

"Great," Liddie said, before my mother could respond. "And when we're done with that, why don't you just give me a boob job? Is there anything else you see wrong with me?"

"I'm sorry," the woman murmured. "I know it's a sensitive subject."

"We were in a little accident a few years back," said my mother. "I think Liddie wants her battle wound."

"It wasn't a little accident," Liddie said.

"She was six," my mother said, as if this proved something about Liddie's reliability.

The truth was we all trusted Liddie's memory, and she knew it. Anytime Liddie wanted a favor from me or wanted our parents' permission for something she had no business doing, she'd lift her hand and push her hair back ever so slightly, so subtly you couldn't call her on it. I blamed her—sometimes—for my mother's cheerful denial of everything that was wrong with us, and for my father's whiskey habit and nightly disappearances into his study. Without her, it might have been easier to forget what had happened. It was Liddie who knew most of all how fixated our father was on the accident, because she regularly brought him coffee and food at night, even during that year when she was boycotting cooking.

"Don't you think he goes in there with the door locked because he wants to be alone?" I'd asked her once when we were teenagers.

"I'm just trying to get his mind off it," she said. According to Liddie, our father had a drawer full of clippings about the accident. Alone in his office, each night, he drank and read them over and over.

"Maybe he wouldn't dwell on it so much if you weren't always throwing it in his face so you could walk all over him," I said. She'd done it at dinner that night: flashed her scar at our parents when they started on her for mouthing off to her history teacher.

She looked at me, exasperated more than angry.

"It's called love, shithead. You hurt people, and then you make it better."

• • •

Every woman in my life had a screwed-up philosophy about love. My mother's was that love was built on a series of unbreakable formalities, which was her excuse for buying me a train ticket from DC to Boston so that Liddie wouldn't spend Thanksgiving alone, which I had understood to be the whole point of her not coming home in the first place. Gabi had spelled hers out in the note she left me:

Terrence,

When I was a kid I had these caterpillars I used to pick up off the sidewalk on the way home from school and keep all over the balcony, in shoeboxes and jelly jars with the tops off. My mother wasn't a fan. Little furry worms, she called them. She always used to say, If you love something, let it go. If it comes back to you it is yours, if it doesn't it was never yours to begin with. She said this especially often once I started with the caterpillars. I think really she just wanted the balcony clean, but at the time I didn't know that and I felt guilty about having them, so after school one day I said good-bye to all the caterpillars and dumped them out of their jars from our fifth-story balcony, where, of course, they fell to their deaths. I am thinking there ought to be a corollary to that set it free thing. If you love something, don't throw it off a balcony. But I'm not quite there yet.

Gabi

That was it. I pictured her as a child, beige and freckled and crying over the smushed and mangled bodies of caterpillars, her eyes

flickering from brown to green the way they did when she was upset.
It seemed like the kind of thing that she would dwell on; though
her childhood was a TV movie waiting to happen, she would blame
her craziness on some dead caterpillars. I thought about tracking her
down, begging her to come back, but I was not given to sweeping
romantic gestures. Anyway, I didn't know where to look. She'd
worked in the bookstore that I managed, pouring overpriced and
watered-down coffee for people too cheap to buy books before reading them. I was so used to her being everywhere I was that I had no
idea where to look for her once she was not. Her coworkers didn't
know where she'd gone, even when I abused my authority as manager to bribe them with shift changes and unearned overtime bonuses.
Really, there was no one else to ask. I was not the first person she'd
disappeared from in her life.

After I got done being angry at her for walking out like that, I
was pissed that she had compared me to a caterpillar— though I had
to admit, hungover and sprawled on the living room carpet, I was
not unlike a spineless insect. It was, I told myself, the suddenness of
the whole thing; sudden for me, anyway. Scanning the bedroom, I
noticed that all of her perfumes and brushes and inexplicable tubes
and creams were gone, that as impulsive as her leaving seemed, she'd
thought about it long enough to pack completely.

It was beautiful in Boston when the train pulled up, and even more
beautiful when I arrived in Harvard Square via rental car. Harvard's
campus seemed designed to demonstrate to outsiders what was

missing in their lives. It was the Wednesday before Thanksgiving, and the Square was much emptier than the other time I'd visited, but the trees were lush with color, and the brick buildings looked almost theatrical. I parked without much trouble and waited for Liddie on a cobblestone corner until she finally appeared wrapped in a brown sweatshirt that was too big and too plain-looking to actually belong to her. Her hair had been dyed some shade of burgundy since I'd seen her last, and she'd lost weight in a way that made her features look sharper.

After confirming that Mom had authorized me to use her credit card for this trip, Liddie dragged me to a Mediterranean restaurant called Casablanca for dinner. It had giant scenes from the movie painted on the walls, and while we gorged ourselves, me on three kinds of chicken, Liddie on dressed-up squash, she dramatically said things like *Well, there are certain sections of New York, Major, that I wouldn't advise you to try to invade* and *You know how you sound, Mr. Blaine? Like a man who's trying to convince himself of something he doesn't believe in his heart.* Mostly she was speaking to her silverware, which both entertained me and kept me from having to make conversation. We were at wine and dessert before she asked me about myself.

"What's with you?" she asked. "Where's wifey?"

"That's a boring story," I said. "What happened to the poet?"

"Broke up with him. He loved me so much, it was starting to get weird. Besides, he wasn't a very good poet." Liddie licked some chocolate off of her spoon. "That was a boring story too. Tell me something interesting."

"Someone's been using my Social Security number to get credit cards," I said.

"I thought *you* couldn't even use your Social Security number to get credit cards anymore," Liddie said.

"That's the thing," I said, "Fucker makes his payments on time more often than I do. The cops said he's probably illegal or something and just needs the number."

"Undocumented," said Liddie, "and there are *cops* involved?"

I told her about my unexpected visitors.

"Aren't you curious?" Liddie asked when I'd finished my story. "I mean, don't you want to find this guy?"

It was moments like this when I remembered why I loved my sister so much: anyone else would have nagged me about the paperwork. Liddie looked like she'd been presented with an early Christmas present and couldn't wait a week to shake it or carefully peel the wrapping.

"His name's Carlos Aguilar," I said, and I didn't mean for there to be anything in my voice when I said it, but Liddie flinched anyway. Then she shrugged.

"There's like fifty billion people named Carlos Aguilar," she said. "He's not ours."

"Of course not," I said, as if the thought had never crossed my mind, maybe like I didn't even remember the name.

It wasn't impossible that I'd forgotten; I deliberately remembered very little about the accident and the years immediately following it. What I remember about the year after the accident is mostly silence:

the silence of our house without the television, which my parents locked in the basement in case I was old enough to connect our accident to the vigils and fund-raisers for the dead children and their surviving family; Liddie's three weeks of complete silence, which caused our parents to call every child psychologist in the New York area; the dinner-table silences as our parents tried not to blame each other; my own silence, because I had no one to talk to; and the silence of my parents' friends and colleagues, who knew it wasn't technically their fault but could not bring themselves to offer condolences.

The children were survived by their bereaved parents and an older child who had not been in the car, Carlos, age ten. They were poor and immigrants and there was a public outcry when the family returned to El Salvador to bury the children and was denied reentry into the country. A popular right-wing talk show host lost his job for saying it served them right for being here illegally and implying they'd been driving poorly because they couldn't read English. There was too much tragedy to be compounded with sympathy for us.

If you were wondering who to blame, it goes like this: The family is driving back from the city, coming around a curve only to find the road blocked by fallen lumber. The father, maybe he looks backward, maybe he thinks about whether he can make it if he swerves, maybe he confers with his wife, but he slows, he stops the car, he gets out to move the wood so they can pass. We are coming around the corner, on our way home from dinner at my aunt's house, and my father does not see them until it is too late. Maybe it happened because the road was curving and poorly lit and no one could have. Maybe I shouldn't have whined that I wanted to stay at my aunt's house until the cartoon I'd been watching was over. Maybe my mother shouldn't have told my father to hurry up so that she could make her church board conference call that evening. Maybe my father, who had been drinking wine with my aunt, but wasn't drunk by any legal standard, should not have had the second glass. Maybe the other father should have swerved around the roadblock. Maybe he should have put his hazards on. Maybe the city should have lit the road better, or maybe it's all the fault of some jackass truck driver who let lumber fall off the back of his truck and drove off scot-free.

The official police report says that it was a no-fault accident, but it is always someone's fault. At the start of high school, they sent me home with this puzzle:

> The king of a vast empire is so impressed with his new and foreign territories that he is hardly home, forgoing the palace to visit the rest of his realm. Lonely, the queen takes a lover, a nobleman in a neighboring town. Not wanting to raise the awareness of the king's loyal guard, she sneaks out of the palace to meet him disguised as a peasant. The guard is aware of this deception, but says nothing and does nothing to stop her. Traveling alone, the queen is attacked and murdered by highway robbers who have no idea who she is. Who is most at fault for the queen's death: the robbers, the guard, the queen, the king, or the lover?

I took the puzzle home and told Liddie about it. I said the robbers were to blame, Liddie picked the queen. The next day, the teacher told our class that who you blamed showed what you valued: justice, duty, faith, love, or family. I thought it was bullshit, and when I got home I lied and told Liddie that the teacher had said she was wrong, that only the robbers were at fault, because only they acted with intent. Liddie shook her head and said that was stupid, the queen probably knew the road was dangerous and anyway the robbers were the only people who didn't owe anybody anything to begin with.

To me the accident is something like that, blame for everyone and no one. A stupid puzzle, not worth solving. My parents never saw it that way. It was a difficult fall and a worse winter. Once Liddie spoke again, my mother began talking to her nonstop, about everything but the accident. Mid-conversation my father would get up and disappear. My mother first threw herself into Christmas with an enthusiasm as profound and suspect as that of department stores. Then she began to yell at us, mostly at me, since everyone else had chosen not to listen. We got used to yelling, and when Becky from the electric company called the morning of Christmas Eve to complain about the bill being late, not because we didn't have the money but because my parents had stopped thinking about that sort of thing, my mother yelled at her too. The difference between being Becky and being anyone else my mother yelled at was that Becky turned off our electricity.

Christmas Day my parents left the dark house early in the morning. They didn't tell us they were leaving, they just walked out and shut the door, and Liddie and I weren't sure whether we had been left on purpose or forgotten. The lights had been out all night, and the food in the refrigerator was starting to go bad. Liddie and I sat in our pajamas, alone, staring at the tree that wouldn't light up. When our parents returned hours later with pizza and Chinese food and flashlights and candles, we exhaled breath we didn't know we'd been holding and ate cold food in the dark silence.

The next summer we moved, hoping for redemption through change of location. My father accepted an offer from Georgetown, where so far as anyone knew he'd always been quiet and eccentric and prone to drinking, not unforgivable traits in a law professor. My mother devoted herself to the kind of ostentatious suburban pursuits that let her pretend we were the ideal family, without actually having to talk to us. She chauffeured us to sport and dance lessons until we were old enough to refuse, she won three homeowner's association bake-offs in a row, and she made such a show of ceremonial occasions that Liddie and I tried to skip our own birthday parties. Even when we had good days, at night it was clear that we had run away from everything except ourselves. Most nights my father was locked in his study, and my mother was knocked out on sleeping pills. Liddie brought her nightmares to me; I did what I could to comfort her. She slept in my bed more often than not until she was twelve and I was fifteen. When I woke one night and found my hand cupped over her breast I shook her awake.

"Liddie," I told her, "you can't sleep here anymore." If my mother, who already looked at us like slightly dangerous strangers, walked in on us curled up in bed together, she'd throw herself off the nearest bridge. Liddie looked at me like I had slapped her. It had never occurred to her that we could be anything but kids together and I had shattered something by the very suggestion, forced her into premature adulthood. She went back to her bed and slept there for the rest of our adolescence, though her nightmares continued; I could hear them through the wall.

At fifteen, she started bringing her boyfriend over and having sex with him in her bedroom. No one stopped her. My father was passed out in his study, and my mother, when she was awake, knew Liddie had more control over the house than she did. I listened to the frantic panting for a few nights, then bought a Walkman with headphones.

Sometimes I thought she'd never forgiven me for not taking some action to save us. For never taking action when I should. She was pleasant enough tonight though, singing "As Time Goes By" off-key all the way back to her dorm room. My mother had refused to pay for a hotel room, on the grounds that if we each had our own spaces we'd probably ruin the point of the visit by confining ourselves to them. It was a rare insight on her part. I dropped my stuff in Liddie's wood-paneled common area and tried to think of something brotherly to say about the formality of her living quarters, but all I could think of to say was, "It's very clean in here."

Liddie ignored me. She'd grabbed a book from out of her bedroom and sat across from me on a beanbag chair, reading furiously and applying yellow Post-it notes to pages. She was sitting between the radiator and the open window, and occasionally a breeze made the pages flutter. Watching her, it seemed even sillier to me that my mother had sent me here to advise Liddie. I had no business telling her anything about how to be a student. When I was in college, I'd lived in an off-campus pigsty and spent most of my free time playing video games. I'd been an OK student, but I did more reading working at the bookstore now than I had back then. I picked up a newspaper and pretended to care about things for a while, then I switched to her suitemate's copy of *Entertainment Weekly* and stared at Beyoncé instead. Liddie muttered to herself about vertebrate bone structure. After about an hour she slammed the book shut.

"Let's find him," she said.

"Who?"

"That guy who wants to be you. Let's confront our curiosity."

There were many reasons why this was a bad idea. I wasn't supposed to take the rental car out of Massachusetts. Even if we left now, it would probably be early tomorrow morning before we arrived in Maryland. When we got there we'd be twenty minutes away from our parents. If we didn't show up, we'd get caught or feel guilty about not getting caught. If we did, there'd be explanations to give; neither of our parents would believe we'd driven nine hours because we missed them. Our curiosity about Carlos was probably not the best motivation for a trip like this. Right then, though, it seemed so easy not to disappoint my sister, and such opportunities were rare.

"You know it's not him, right?" I said.

"Of course," Liddie said. "But I want to know who it *is*. I mean, who wants our lives?"

I hadn't unpacked anything, and Liddie hadn't bothered to pack at all, so it was only an hour later that we found ourselves headed south on the interstate. It was already after midnight, and the roads were emptier than I had expected. People had either done their leaving already or they were waiting until the last possible minute. The weather was clear, and you could even see stars, which felt like a good omen. Liddie fiddled with the radio until she found a jazz station and then continued reading her textbook with a flashlight. We were just outside of Hartford when she finally shut it.

"So, Gabi," said Liddie.

"She left me."

"Obviously."

"I could have left her."

"No," Liddie said, not obnoxiously. "No, you couldn't have."

"I *could* have," I said. "I just wouldn't have."

Liddie didn't respond.

"So," I said finally. "The elephants. What's so amazing about them that they need my sister as their shrink?"

"Lots of things. They're so much like us. Elephant society has been breaking down just like ours has. Increased violence. Pack violence, even. They experience shock. They've got elaborate grieving rituals, like humans. I guess that's why they always seemed sad to me."

"Always?"

"I used to go to the zoo sometimes in high school. It was calming." A minute later she said softly, "Let's go see them. The elephants. Before we look for Carlos, I mean."

She turned to look at me with very big eyes, and very lightly brushed her hair off her forehead. I knew what she was doing, but it was working anyway.

"Liddie," I said, "it's Thanksgiving."

"The National Zoo is open every day of the year except Christmas."

"That's ridiculous," I said.

"We're in a car going back where you just came from to find a guy who's improving your credit by using your name illegally because we think somehow he might be a guy we didn't kill, and he might be as obsessed with us as we are with him, just because he's got like the second most common name in the world. *That's* ridiculous."

"Hey, that was your idea too," I said.

"It was your idea first. You just wouldn't have gone through with it."

As usual, I caved. Content, Liddie fell asleep for a while. Outside of Maryland I pulled over for a second, and she woke up and took over driving, which was maybe the fourth thing in the car rental contract that I'd violated. It was a little after nine when we pulled into the zoo's parking lot. I'd been trying for an hour to stay asleep in spite of the sun prying at my eyes. I was surprised the zoo was open that early, but Liddie seemed confident it would be, which was the first thing that convinced me she wasn't bullshitting me about hanging out here in high school.

We went straight for the elephants, but even they seemed to know that it was a holiday and they didn't need to be awake yet. There were three of them, two adults and a baby. We watched them sleep for a while, and I tried to see something magical about it, but I didn't. I looked at the other early-morning zoo weirdos and tried to imagine what we looked like to them. There was a wan-looking art student with long blond hair, sketching the sleeping elephants on a giant pad. There was a man in uniform with a little girl on his shoulders. There was a teenager who looked like he was either homeless or that was how he wanted to look; eventually his cell phone rang and I figured it was the latter. There was a middle-aged woman in a nice coat that was too thin for the November weather. She reminded me of Gabi, though she was older and less pretty. Something about the calculated vulnerability of her shivering when she didn't have to.

None of the strangers seemed interested in me. The teenager checked out Liddie briefly but then went back to walking around in circles. One of the elephants got up eventually and wandered off where we couldn't see her. The other two kept sleeping.

"You're right," I said to Liddie. "They're fascinating."

"They *are*," Liddie insisted. "What do you think the sleeping one's dreaming about?"

"Peanuts," I said.

"Don't be a dumb-ass," said Liddie. "I bet he's dreaming about his mother, who was killed by ivory poachers in front of him, and he's wishing he'd been big enough to trample the men and save her."

"I bet Mom and Dad are sorry they read you *Babar* when you were a kid," I said.

"That wasn't Mom and Dad, that was you," she said. "I don't know why you were reading me that colonialist bullshit anyway."

"Is that what this is about?" I joked. "That I raised you badly?"

"No," she said. "I think as long as you get raised, it can't count as badly."

I disagreed, but didn't say so.

We spent a few more hours at the zoo, just wandering around, looking at the stray people and occasional families. Around one we ate lunch at a downtown McDonald's. It was sad how crowded it was. There were paper turkey cutouts stuck to the windows. I ate two Big Macs while Liddie picked at her french fries and neglected to say anything about any of the ways McDonald's exploited people, which is how I knew she was getting antsy. Our mother called around two. I could hear the television in the background, the too-cheery voice of morning TV anchors. It was the Macy's parade, I realized; my mother must have taped it and was watching it again. It made me a little bit sad and a little bit angry.

"How are you two doing?" she asked, in her voice straining to sound happy.

"Great," I said, "just great. We're cooking things now, in the common-room kitchen. The chicken smells wonderful."

This seemed to me the biggest lie of all, since we were still in McDonald's and everything smelled like grease and plastic.

"How are Liddie's studies coming?" Mom asked.

"Fantastic," I said. "Today she taught me about elephants."

"You haven't tried to talk her out of that nonsense?"

"I have never talked her out of anything. That's why she talks to me."

Liddie rolled her eyes at this and grabbed my cell phone.

"Mo-om," she said. "It's a holiday. We're festive. Can't we just stay festive?"

I could hear through the phone my mother trying to sound conciliatory, but I could see on Liddie's face that she could hear the taped parade in the background too. Her tone got softer and sadder when she said good-bye.

After she hung up, I got a milk shake and Liddie ordered some pitiful-looking granola without the yogurt. When we'd wasted all the time we could, we got back in the car and headed for Maryland, to the address I'd confirmed and written down before we left Cambridge. We were quiet, and ashamed of ourselves on many counts.

We found where we were going quickly. It really was right over the bridge. It was a garden apartment complex, everything low to the ground and in the same shade of dull red brick. There were already Christmas lights strung across some of the balconies, and there was music coming from several different parked cars: Nas on one side, something with the same bass in a different language on the other. I parked right in front of the building and turned off the engine. Liddie and I sat in the car like criminals preparing for a heist. I couldn't tell from the outside which of the apartments in the building might be Carlos's. We watched people come and go for a while, many of them carrying aluminum-covered dishes. A harried woman in a uniform rushed in, almost tripping over two kids playing with toy cars on the steps. A few feet from the front stoop a teenage couple kissed a passionate good-bye, the boy's hands inching slowly down the girl's waist before she caught them with manicured pink fingertips and raised his grip back to safer territory.

A woman laughed loudly at the spectacle, her stilettos clicking against the ground as she walked. She walked confidently, her hips swinging, her hair tossing backward in soft curls. There was a baby in her arms; it bounced with the rhythm of her walking. Everything about her seemed musical. Beneath the apartment building's front awning, she paused, shifting the baby and fumbling for her keys. The orange light above her made her look alien, but still pretty. She turned and called behind her, "Carlos!"

At the other end of the sidewalk, two men obscured by shadows looked up at the sound of her voice. I looked in their direction, waiting to see who responded. Neither of them looked anything like the Carlos Aguilar in the picture we'd seen in the paper. He'd been much darker than either of the men I was looking at; his features, even as a kid, had been sharper. I watched the men carefully anyway. I wondered which of them would hug the woman, and which of them would hold the baby, and what the woman and the baby would smell like up close, feel like to touch. I wondered if either of the men had what he wanted, if either of them could have been me in another life.

"Let's go home," I said to Liddie, who was watching the woman intently.

"Yeah," she said.

I knew she'd understood me when I turned south toward

Virginia, instead of north toward Boston, and she didn't register any surprise. She played with the car CD player until Mingus wailed sadly in the background. I stopped at a Chinese take-out place and ordered dinner. Walking back to the parking lot, with the warm bag of food in my arms, I saw Liddie sitting in the car, the sideways light of the setting sun making her scar glow. We were what we had in life, I thought, and I was not sad about it or apologetic for its corniness. We drove the last five minutes home, where both of our parents' cars were in the driveway but the blinds were drawn. I pictured my parents as I knew we'd find them, alone in the quickly darkening house, sitting next to each other on the couch and imagining everyone else's family while the television lied to them. I pictured them being lonely without us on one of the few days a year we were promised to them. Liddie and I got out of the car and stood on the front porch, bracing ourselves for the sound of the doorbell.

Jellyfish

The roof of William's Harlem apartment building fell in on a Wednesday, three weeks before he was due to renew his lease. Everyone seemed to think it was a sign of something. Janice in 2F thought the landlord caved the roof in on purpose, to chase out the last of the rent-controlled tenants. Ed, the eighty-something widower two flights down, thought it was an accident on the part of the city, something gone wrong while they were covertly practicing riot-control tactics. The kids next door pasted fliers around the block, claiming the damage was the result of a minor earthquake caused by global warming. Phil, the landlord, said it was a pipe bursting in the empty apartment beside William's, but in any case, when the wall went, it took the chunk of roof directly above William's living room with it, leaving a large pile of rubble atop the remnants of his glass coffee table and a thin film of white dust over all of his belongings.

He barely had time to get home from the office and survey the damage before the city showed up and declared the whole building structurally unsound and an asbestos hazard. He was given forty-eight hours to take what he could and be elsewhere before they sealed most of his life behind yellow tape. After turning down Phil's offer of a temporary basement apartment ten blocks uptown, William broke out his emergency credit card, relocated himself to a midtown hotel, and reluctantly called a broker about a new apartment.

"I don't know why you didn't move a long time ago," said his ex-wife, Debra, when he called to tell her about it. "It's a wonder it's only now falling down. That rat trap was only supposed to be temporary when you moved in twenty years ago."

"Twenty years ago, I was still under the impression that *our marriage* was *not* supposed to be temporary," he snapped back. "Besides, welcome to the new Harlem. I've lived here so long that everyone *wants* to live in my neighborhood again."

"Not without roofs, they don't," said Debra, and after a week of stubborn resistance to everything the broker showed him, William was forced to concede the point.

Two weeks after her father's roof fell in, Eva woke up to the blaring alarm of her cell phone, reminding her of the lunch date she'd programmed into her phone a few days earlier. She blinked at a crack in the ceiling, momentarily worried that her own roof was caving in out of solidarity, before rubbing the sleep from her eyes. It was not her ceiling she was looking at, she realized. It was not her bed that she was in, and it hadn't been her apartment in over a year. Cheese was still asleep, and though it occurred to her to wake him so he wouldn't be late for his shift at the coffee shop, she tiptoed to the shower instead, hoping to be ready to leave by the time he woke up so they wouldn't have to talk about what she was doing there for the third time this week. After a few minutes of futilely turning the shower dials in search of heat or water pressure, Eva stumbled out smelling like another woman's grapefruit and lily soap. Her damp curls made her grateful, at least, that she hadn't bothered straightening her hair for her father's benefit.

After fumbling through her backpack for something that wasn't dirty, flecked with clay from her studio, or otherwise likely to offend her father, she gave up. Eva started on Cheese's wardrobe, looking for something that didn't scream that she'd spent the night at her ex-boyfriend's apartment. When that didn't work, she reminded herself that Cheese's current girlfriend was in another state, ostensibly working up the energy to break up with him, and went through what was left on the girlfriend's side of the closet, finally finding a button-down dress that was clean and high-collared and respectable. She noted, with equal parts contempt and admiration, that Cheese's latest girlfriend was the sort of girl who ironed and kept things creased where they were supposed to be. She noted also, while buttoning, how easily the dress slipped over her hips. There had been a note of genuine concern in Cheese's voice when he pointed out how thin she'd gotten and asked her if she was still eating OK. She told him that she was, a mostly honest answer: she was eating less lately only because living alone made the awkwardness of keeping to regular mealtimes almost unbearable. The soft worry of his voice when he'd asked was at odds with the present. Cheese, now awake, was demanding to know why Eva was wearing Kate's dress.

"Oh, come on," she said, turning around to stare pointedly at his bare chest above the white bedsheet, the faint red tooth marks she'd left beneath his collarbone last night.

"You can't take her dress," he said.

"I'm not taking it, I'm borrowing. And I'm running late. You can yell at me later."

"Is there going to be a later?" he asked. He climbed out of bed, stopping to pick up the armful of bangle bracelets she'd left on the nightstand and hand them to her. "And what are you in such a hurry for, anyway? I thought you said your dad was always late."

It was true, she had said that. Her father was never where he said he'd be when he said he'd be there. When she was small, she would wait on her mother's kitchen windowsill for hours on visiting days, nose pressed against the glass. Her mother would linger in the kitchen looking disapproving, reminding her that it could be hours. It was before everyone carried a cell phone and was always and every minute reachable, and even now Eva hesitated to call her father when she couldn't find him. She preferred when he materialized without preface. Back then she'd leave the windowsill before he arrived, partly out of embarrassment and partly because she knew it would make him sad to see her there, waiting. Once she'd curled up in the window and slept there, intent upon looking pitiful when he arrived, a day later than he had said. When the yellow cab pulled up the next morning, she watched her father exiting the car, saw the genuine smile on his face as he approached the house, and abandoned the operation. She told Cheese this story while she pulled her hair back into some semblance of order and dabbed herself with the perfume vial in her purse, noting that it clashed with the lingering lily scent of soap.

"You sound like me the week after you left me the first time," said Cheese. "I thought every woman walking beneath the window was you."

"Well," said Eva. "Here I am."

"You are," said Cheese. "And I'm sure your father will be there on time today. You said he really wanted to see you, right?"

The worried tone of his question made her want to kiss him, and then to laugh at him, but mostly it made her want to call Maya, the woman for whom she'd left him. It had been two weeks since she'd gotten the last of her belongings from the apartment she and Maya had shared, and they hadn't spoken since. Cheese's tolerance exhausted Eva sometimes. She knew Maya would tell her when she was full of shit. *Avoiding confrontation because you'd rather take shit than deal with it doesn't make you a martyr,* Maya had said to her once, and probably would have said to her again if Eva had tried that windowsill story on her. But Eva didn't bother trying to explain her childhood to Maya; it hadn't been happy exactly, but it hadn't been sad in any way Maya would have understood. On Maya's scale of childhood tragedy, Eva didn't register.

Usually, Eva thought of herself as a good person. She stayed up at night worrying about the human condition in vague and specific incarnations. She made herself available to the people whom she loved, and some whom she didn't. She gave money to every other homeless person and stopped to let stray kids remind her how much Jesus and the Hare Krishnas loved her, more for the benefit of their souls than hers. Still, she wondered sometimes if it wasn't all pretense—if, when she shut her eyes and wished restitution upon the whole wounded parade of humanity, she wasn't really wishing away the world that created war and illness so that she might have a world in which there was room to feel sorry for herself. Every day she felt herself losing things it was unacceptable to mourn.

William was uptown, arguing with Phil about a blender. William had known Phil since moving back to the city in the eighties. Back then, his had been the only building Phil owned, and Phil had lived downstairs and done most of the maintenance himself, but the rapidly rising rents over the past decade, the slick face-lift of 125th Street, and the influx of people no longer scared to live north of it, had made it possible for Phil to expand his operations. He now owned a few older buildings on Convent Avenue, and one on St. Nick; he had moved himself to a brownstone and grown a belly, now that he no longer climbed the stairs to respond to tenants' complaints. William liked Phil, always had. After all those times going to see an available apartment, only to be told the second the owner saw his face that it was suddenly rented, it had been a relief to have a black landlord. Over the years, he and Phil had developed a friendly rapport, met for a drink from time to time even after Phil moved. But now, as Phil stubbornly refused to let him back into the old building to get the blender he'd left unopened in a box in a closet, William was reminded of what Phil had said about the black contractor who'd ripped him off once: *Used to be you could at least count on your own people.*

"I understand," Phil was saying, which of course he did not. "I'd let you in if I could, but it's not up to me. Right now, the city says, *Jump,* I say, *How high?* And the city says, *Nobody goes into that building, and nobody takes anything out,* and I don't take that padlock off the door. Structurally unsound. Breathing hazard. You name it. I start handing out keys because people want to get in and get stuff, next thing you know, the rest of the roof's collapsing or people are squatting in their old apartments, and then the city's shutting down everything else I own."

"Phil," William said, "that's nonsense. You know I'm not moving in. What I just paid for the deposit on my new place, they'll have to bury me there. I just want my stuff. Just the little stuff. I'm late for lunch with my daughter.

"I forgot you had a daughter," said Phil. "I remember her now. Pretty girl."

Eva had not been running late for lunch, so much as running away from Cheese. She knew her father would be at least twenty minutes late, but her arrival at the restaurant fifteen minutes early gave her time to order a gin and tonic. The waiter was young and aggressively charming. Eva asked for extra lemon for her water; he brought her a dish of lemons, and a fresh mint leaf, along with her drink. He hovered. Eva envied his eyelashes. It was not quite lunchtime, and the restaurant was quiet and near empty. It had been a favorite of her father's when he worked nearby, before he'd left his job at the downtown EEOC office for work with a private firm. It would have been easier to meet in midtown, but even after winning several big cases her father didn't seem quite comfortable in his new office, with its smooth burgundy leather and gold-plated doors. He'd liked it better downtown. He used to bring her to this restaurant on visiting days. Eva remembered tapping her Mary Janes against the hardwood floor, getting free Shirley Temples from the old owner. The name of the place was the same now, but the menu had changed from solidly Greek to vaguely Mediterranean, and when Eva asked the waiter how the old owner was doing, he seemed apologetically confused by the fact that the restaurant had ever been anything different.

As he walked away, Eva emptied the contents of a sugar packet onto her teaspoon and swallowed. She assumed this was only rude when someone was watching. Her father was not watching, because he was, according to her intuition and the metallic clock on the wall, still a good fifteen minutes away. She sipped her drink and studied the salad page. A woman in heels walked into the restaurant. *Click, click, click.* The sound of her reminded Eva of Maya, who thought herself short and wore heels even in her own apartment. Maya, whose steps had a perfectly measured rhythm to them. That was what Eva had first noticed when they'd met in the bookstore: the sound of her walking. Maya was brilliant, had a dot-shaped birthmark in the center of her forehead, and was one of the few people Eva knew who still believed in anything, but Eva would have loved her on the basis of sound alone. She instinctively looked up from her table when the woman entered, but only the sound of her was familiar. This woman was skinny and mousy, where Maya was all curve and bravado. The woman sat at the bar and whispered something to the bartender, who seemed to know her. There was a television at the bar, tuned to CNN. A man in a lab coat stood over a kitten, who chased the string he dangled. The kitten was calico and unnaturally small. Eva squinted at the caption.

"Pretty soon they'll be cloning us," the waiter said, while refilling Eva's water glass.

"Well, that's a shame," said Eva. "It's dying."

She did not know this to be true. She remembered reading something about sheep dying. Cloned cells were as old as the parent cells they'd come from. But she had read this in college, some years ago, and it was possible that things had changed since then. Progressed. She watched the kitten swatting at its toy, and bit into a piece of warm bread. *Run, damn you*, Eva thought. The kitten kept swatting at the string. The newsmen pretended to be awed. Eva winked at the waiter and asked for another drink. He nodded, taking the opportunity to glance down her dress.

The blender is not just a blender. It cuts and dices and purees. Eva liked to cook, William had thought when he bought it. When she visited him, which she hadn't recently, she opened his refrigerator and looked disappointed to find it full of take-out cartons. She'd walk him to the downtown grocery, though left to his own devices, if he shopped at all, it would be right down the block at C-Town, the fluorescent light and big red discount signs less disorienting than the cramped aisles, dark lighting, and six-dollar heads of lettuce at the store Eva preferred. She'd make him buy food for himself, remind him that it had been a long time since he couldn't afford to eat better. By the time she'd finished filling baskets with dried pasta and fresh vegetables and jars of floating artichokes, they had so much food they had to take a cab back, food it took him months to entirely dispense with.

Back at his apartment, she'd make elaborate salads and stir-fried vegetables and pasta that always seemed to him a touch undercooked. She'd cut vegetables into thin slivers and squirt them with fresh lemon and tahini. It was watching her cut that made him think of the blender a few months ago. He'd searched for the right one online, evaluating the photos and assorted specifics of blender after blender the way you might compare real estate or personal ads. It would make her life easier. Maybe she would cook at her apartment and think of him while pureeing soup. She would pick up the phone and invite him for dinner. He'd imagined arriving just in time for dinner, finding the table set with her mismatched and brightly colored dishes. He'd imagined eating salads with perfectly julienned carrots.

Thinking it through, though, even if Phil let him in, he should probably leave the blender. Contamination, and all that. Besides, Eva was the type to dwell on things: she'd look at the blender and start talking about the old apartment, or gentrification, or the way they were all slowly dying of chemical poisoning. She'd never cook with it. She'd put it in a closet, or she'd take it to her studio and mount it on one of her sculptures, fence it in with chicken wire. Better that he just buy her another and hope she didn't remember it was a replacement for the first one he'd promised her. Besides, he'd be buying himself a whole new set of kitchen supplies anyway; if Eva would come to stay with him for a bit, she wouldn't need her own. He'd make sure she had everything she wanted; the kitchen in the new place was small, but sunny, and he'd let her pick what it was she needed. Better that he wait to see what she said this afternoon before he gave her one more thing to cart to Brooklyn.

The waiter returned with Eva's second drink. Her father had told her this was a celebratory lunch, she reasoned, though he hadn't said what it was a celebration for. Eva was still watching the television, but between the volume on low and the woman at the bar tipsy and giggling, she couldn't hear a word. The president was mouthing something from behind a podium, and she supposed she didn't care.

"What happened to our kitten?" the waiter asked.

"Dick Cheney ate him," said Eva.

The waiter laughed.

"Are you still waiting to order?" He nodded toward the empty chair.

Eva blushed, realizing she looked for all the world like a woman being stood up for a lunch date. It had been so many years since Eva had been without at least one lover on call that she was surprised by

how quickly awkwardness could come back to her. Now she had the
sense again that anyone could just by looking at her see that she did
not belong to anyone, anywhere. Until the last few years of her life,
when she'd gone flinging herself from lover to lover like a pinball,
she'd considered her not-belonging a badge of honor rather than a
source of shame. It had been the rallying cry of her motley crew
of high school friends—Kim, the purple-haired girl in tortoiseshell
glasses and leopard-print leggings; Lenny, who'd known he was gay
before most of them knew the word as anything but an all-purpose
pejorative; Irene, the only other black girl in her suburban private
school class—they'd sit together at lunch and watch the petty dramas
of their classmates and say out loud, *Who wants that? Who wants those
people, anyway?* But high school had turned into college and then
the handful of years afterward—Kim was living in Cameroon with
the Peace Corps; Lenny was a lawyer in San Francisco; and Irene
was busy playing Gallant to Eva's Goofus in their parents' black
professional circles—working for an investment bank, appearing
regularly at AKA charity events in designer suits, her doctor fiancé
at her side.

While all the others had turned into more self-possessed versions
of themselves, Eva felt further than ever from her old self. Where
once she'd taken her self-sufficiency for granted, somewhere in a dizzying string of morning afters she had started to feel her aloneness
was a mark of incompletion, faintly spreading.

"I'm waiting for my father," Eva said to the waiter, who seemed
ready to snatch away the second menu. "He'll be here. He'll be late,
but he turns up eventually."

She pulled out her cell phone and feigned a search for a text message; the waiter wandered off and left her to her pretense of human interaction.

"Phil," said William, "I lived in that apartment for twenty years. I grew up in the Bronx. If breathing debris hasn't killed me yet, it won't, ever. Explain to me why the city that still hasn't gotten all the asbestos out of its own damn public housing and rents the Bronx out for landfill space is suddenly so concerned about my lungs."

"I'm not the city," said Phil. "Explaining is not my job. You really just want a few photographs?"

"That's all," said William.

Phil motioned him down the block, and they began the short walk from Phil's place to the old building. They cut through the City College campus, and when they got to the other side, Phil stopped for a coffee at the corner store and, while stirring three sugars into it, said with his back to William, "Can I ask you something?"

"Shoot."

"This irreplaceable stuff you need me to open the building so badly so you can get—why didn't you take it with you when they told everybody to get what they were going to get and get out?"

William didn't answer until they were halfway down the block. He considered pretending he hadn't heard the question. Finally he let out a breath and said, "The truth is, I forgot it was there."

William told himself that forgetting something didn't mean you'd forgotten the person associated with it. His own mother, he reminded himself, never could keep up with photographs, wouldn't have expected a drawing to last a week in a two-bedroom apartment with four kids in it, let alone tried to keep it for twenty years. But then, there were four of them, and she had two thirty-hour-a-week jobs, and still she checked in with them every night, still he remembered the cocoa-butter smell of her kissing him good night, and still he sensed that if something had been the only reminder of how things used to be, she never would have forgotten it—not even during all those trash-bag moves from place to place before they got settled. Yet, he couldn't remember to take one box in a closet.

Phil cleared his throat; they were standing in front of the old apartment. Phil looked over his shoulder, as if any one of the kids on the steps across the street might be an undercover city housing operative, then released the chain and padlock from the door and stepped aside.

"I'm waiting for you for fifteen minutes," he said. "Something falls on your head and knocks you out, I'm telling the cops you're a fool and I don't know you."

William walked up the creaky staircase to the third floor, fast for the first two levels, then wondered if one shouldn't walk gingerly in a building people kept threatening was going to fall. He went straight for the closet, left the blender in spite of himself, and pulled out the box in the back of the closet. Most of the things in the box used to be in his office, but when he'd moved up in the world—literally up—he'd brought the box home, instead of to the new place. In his new office, he had only two pictures of Eva, including the most recent picture she had given him: her in a park somewhere, smiling at he probably didn't even want to know who, the streaks in her hair a shade of fluorescent red like the color of the lighted trim on an old jukebox.

But the old boxes, they were full of pictures of his daughter the way he remembered her. Debra had sent him one for every school year, plus one for every recital, plus an annual Christmas picture taken on the steps of the church Eva had refused to attend once she turned sixteen. Debra had mailed them meticulously to everyone at the holidays, letting Eva cut the wallet-sized photos along their white lines by herself (he could see the jagged edges on the early photos). He wanted to display these things again, he thought, to display them where Eva could see them.

From just after the divorce until Eva was a teenager, Debra had dropped her off one Friday afternoon each month, spent the weekend with friends in the city, and come to collect her Sunday morning. William still had seven years' worth of those Friday-afternoon visits stored up in the box. Fridays must have been art days at school; he had all sorts of odd ceramic and papier-mâché animals, though he suspected he had only the ugly ones, the ones that Debra didn't want. Dogs without legs and the like. He was more fond of the paper: years' worth of elaborate abstract drawings Eva made by coloring over interoffice memos in red, black, and blue pen, the scribbled-on pages she had ripped out of coloring books and left with him.

He pulled out one crinkled page from the corner of the box where it had been jammed. It was from the year of the self-esteem books, the year after he'd showed up for Eva's eighth-birthday party and found that the guests were all eleven-year-olds. Debra swore she'd get to the bottom of it, and indeed she had. Eva, it seemed, had begun spending lunch and recess with the fifth-graders, after the third-grade bully called her a nigger and told her she couldn't sit at the lunch table. *William, we have to do something about this*, Debra had said. Her first solution was to take an early lunch hour and accompany Eva to the cafeteria every day, a plan that Eva had promptly vetoed. Next she swore they were moving. *Where*, William had asked, *to another planet?*

In the end, Debra had purchased a year's worth of coloring books with names like *I am Beautiful* and *Why I Love Myself*, the idea being that Eva could learn to be her own champion. He had tried to talk to Eva about all of it once, but all she would say was that she wished her mother hadn't told the lunch monitors what was going on, because she liked the fifth-graders better. She had given him that page, the page she was coloring at the time. It began: *I am special because . . .* and had lines, presumably for listing the conditions of one's specialness. Eva had ignored the lines and finished the sentence: *I am just special. I am special because I am just special*. There was Eva, he thought, not unkindly. There was Eva, and what did you do with a girl like that? William collected himself, sealed the box as best he could, then went downstairs to assure Phil he was uninjured, and hail the first cab going downtown.

Eva heard the door jingle as her father walked into the restaurant. She took a sip of water so that he wouldn't smell her breath and know that she'd been drinking. She wasn't sure why she got that way around him, guilty about things she had no reason to be ashamed of, but that was how it was.

"Hello, beautiful," he said, kissing the top of her head and sitting across from her.

She smiled across the table, then looked curiously at the box he had set down beside them. She had long ceased to be amazed by her father's lateness, but admired that his reasons were always surprising, involving some unsuspected feat he had undertaken while most of the late people in the world were missing trains or sleeping through alarms.

"What's in the box, Daddy?"

"In this box," he said grinning, "are the fruits of a morning's labor." He told the story of his morning uptown.

"Poor Phil," said Eva. "Bad enough his building got condemned, now he'll have nightmares about ceramic animals living in it."

"It was me the building almost fell down on," her father said. "Don't go feeling too sorry for Phil."

"I'm sorry, Daddy. Is everything OK? Mom said they weren't going to let you get all of your things back."

"Your mother knows better than to think I'd give up that easy. Like I was going to leave all this for the city to burn?" He reached into the box and pulled out the first solid object, a framed picture of Eva after a tap recital. Her hair was teased into glossy curls, and she was wearing the kind of stage makeup that makes children look garish up close.

"I'm going to put these up in the new—"

"God," said Eva, staring at the photo, "I look like JonBenét Ramsey."

She flinched at her own lack of social grace and continued, "I'm sorry, Daddy. I didn't mean—What were you saying?"

But her father was saying nothing now. He looked at her, confused, and they let the awkward silence sit until the waiter came to rescue them.

"So," her father asked, once they had ordered, "how are things? You look lovely, by the way. That's a beautiful dress."

It was unfair of him to ask how she was doing. William knew more than he let on. He knew, for example, that she could probably use extra money. Eva had put on one gallery show, in a deliberately spare gallery on a side street in Chelsea. The art paid infrequently; she worked other jobs to support herself. She did paperwork for an art museum. Weekends, she worked in a store that sold sex toys. When Debra told him this, he thought she was kidding, but it was true. It's also a bookstore, Debra said, by way of consolation. He went to the store once, to see it for himself. The windows were papered in red and when he opened the door he was confronted with a table full of vibrators. He shut it quickly. Sometimes he thought her whole life was an elaborate series of barricades against him.

He knew about the girlfriend, though even Debra seemed uncertain about the current status of this relationship. They were not "roommates" anymore, but he was not sure what this meant, considering they were hardly roommates to begin with. He knew that Eva had been living in her own small studio for the past month, though a few years ago when he'd asked why she couldn't just get a bigger place instead of paying rent in two places, neither especially nice, she'd insisted that she couldn't sleep where she worked. She'd been living with her boyfriend at the time. When he'd brought this up with Debra, Debra said, *She just didn't want to tell you that Cheese isn't making her pay rent.* He had laughed at the absurdity of this deception. His daughter was dating a white boy with three earrings and a tattoo he said was symbolic of the Great Gatsby, a boy who insisted on going by his high school nickname of "Cheese" when his parents had given him the perfectly sensible name of Charles, and what Eva found most embarrassing was that she wasn't paying any rent to live with him.

He wondered if Eva really thought he didn't know these things, whether the charade was for his benefit or hers. Aside from being her father, he dealt with liars for a living, and Eva was no actress. He was not certain whether Eva had fully come to terms with her mother's inability to keep secrets. Most likely, she just didn't imagine that they still talked as often as they did. It made him sad sometimes to think that Eva maybe couldn't understand this, the kind of bond you never lose. It was true, he had blamed Debra for things. He had plans, rules, which were disrupted in the first place by Debra leaving him, and in the second place by Eva herself. He'd had speeches and punishments prepared for the normal things: dating, drugs, slacking in school. Eva never seemed to get in trouble for the normal things. In high school she'd been arrested at a protest for standing too close to a group of kids throwing eggs at the cops. He didn't have a speech for that. Only once had he gotten a call from the school. Debra was away at a conference and he had taken his vacation time to stay with Eva for the week. *Could someone come get Eva?* the secretary had said. She'd been suspended for biting another student.

"Biting?" he'd asked. Eva was a sophomore in high school. He hadn't known fifteen-year-olds bit people.

"Biting," the secretary had confirmed, so he'd gone to the school to sort things out. There wasn't much sorting. Eva confessed to the biting and could offer no better reason than that the boy had been getting on her nerves.

"I value silence," she'd said, "and he wouldn't shut up."

He'd had no choice but to take her back to the house and wait for Debra to get back that evening. Debra had gone to the school the next day, the first day of Eva's suspension, and demanded further questioning of the boy. He eventually admitted to having grabbed Eva's behind earlier in the day. Debra threatened the boy, the school, and the parents, and Eva's suspension was reversed.

"Why didn't you tell me he touched you?" William asked Eva later.

"Didn't matter," she'd said. "That wasn't why I bit him."

The arrival of her salad saved Eva from further strained conversation about the state of her life. She'd already claimed, "I like living in the studio," and "I'm getting so much work done." She crunched on a crouton.

"I'm glad to see you eating," her father said.

Eva sighed. "Daddy I've been eating for years. We eat together sometimes."

"I know," he said. "I'm just saying. You look good. Healthy."

She was certain that her mother had encouraged him to say this sort of thing. Eva wished there were a Bat-Signal for the waiter, something to invite him to disrupt them. She hated the inexplicable things between them, the secrets her mother had given away, even though they weren't hers to keep. She remembered all those school picture days and holidays and recitals, and she liked it better when her father thought of her that way. These days she couldn't be around him without feeling that, without thinking he was waiting for her to win something and smile pretty.

She stabbed a tomato. She'd been eating normally since junior year of college, since she'd broken up with the last boyfriend her father had actually liked, the charming premed who'd told her she had cellulite and pretended not to hear when she threw up in his bathroom. He'd asked about that boyfriend all the time she was with Cheese, and twice as often when she was with Maya, until one day she'd said without explaining, *Do you want me to hate myself?* after which he'd never asked again.

When she was being honest with herself, which was more often than she was honest with other people, she admitted that Cheese was the first boy who'd ever made her feel beautiful, the first man in her life she was sure was never going anywhere no matter what she did, not that it kept her from testing him. When she talked to Lenny on the phone, or replied to Kim's sporadic e-mails, or met Irene for drinks, dinner, and conversations that felt increasingly obligatory, she gave them a host of quite rational reasons for why she and Cheese would never really get back together. He was twenty-eight years old and seemed content to be a barista forever; he claimed to love her art but resented the time she spent on it; she had been the first of what was now a line of four artsy ethnic girlfriends in a row, making her feel a bit like he was collecting them the way her old ceramics instructor collected dolls of the world. But the truth was there was something about his availability that unsettled her, that made her want to know what it would finally take for him not to be there when she showed up unannounced.

She'd done it a month ago, the night she and Maya had broken up—thought maybe this time he would finally tell her she couldn't do this to him anymore, that they both had to move on—but he'd opened the door and let her in. The girlfriend was still living in the apartment then, but she'd been gone for the weekend, meaning Eva got to curl herself into the corner of the saggy orange sofa she and Cheese had gotten for free off of craigslist two years earlier, and drink the cheap bourbon he poured her a shot of, and tell him what had happened.

What had happened, first, was that she and Maya had redecorated, taken to painting the walls in brightly contrasting colors, and then hanging brightly printed fabrics on the wall: red against the kitchen's deep purple, orange against the green of the bedroom. What had happened a few days after the apartment's transformation was Eva thought of the stark, yellowing walls of her father's cramped apartment, the faintly moldy smell of them, the way he shrugged off her gentle suggestions that there were plenty of nicer places he could afford to move; he didn't even have to leave the neighborhood. He would offer some excuse about the hassle of getting the couch down the narrow stairwell without ruining it, as if he couldn't afford new furniture these days, or about liking his landlord, as if Phil would hold it against him if he moved out of a building that Phil himself had left years ago. But she never pressed, because under the flimsy excuses she guessed her father's reasoning was something along the lines of *Why bother?* He saw most of the people he wanted to see at work, had built a network of friends who spent more time at the office than at their own homes anyway. The only person who came to see him on a semi-regular basis was Eva, and although there were only thirty blocks between them—eight subway stops, counting the back-tracking, but walkable, if you were in the mood for walking—it had been over a month since she'd last been to visit, and she almost never invited him to visit her.

When Maya floated in from work, *click-clicking* against the floors, smelling vaguely honeyed from her shampoo and mildly sweaty from her bike ride home from the after-school center where she was a social worker, Eva had already been shopping, planned a menu, bought decent wine instead of the cheap stuff she and Maya usually drank, and was a minute away from inviting her father over for dinner the next night, giving him time to get home before she called.

"What's the occasion?" Maya asked. She dropped her shoulder bag on the kitchen counter and held Eva around the waist, planting a soft kiss on the side of her neck.

"I'm inviting my dad over for dinner tomorrow," said Eva. She could feel Maya's arms stiffen, then drop from around her.

"Great," said Maya. Her shoes clicked backward, away from Eva. Eva turned to face her, watched her arms fold across her body. "Does that mean I have to make plans elsewhere?"

"Who said that?"

"Your father hates me."

"He doesn't. He just doesn't understand—us."

"Maybe he'd understand better if you stopped introducing me as your roommate. He knows you're bullshitting him."

"Maya—I'm trying. Everybody's parents aren't so awful that they can tell them to go fuck themselves and move on with their lives, and everybody doesn't have a foster mom who owns a berry farm upstate and makes her own tie-dye skirts and is thrilled to meet her daughter's girlfriend. He's lonely, and he's my father, and he's never done anything *bad* to you. To me, either, for that matter."

"Is that the standard for parenting these days?"

"Maya, don't. I don't need you to fix this. I'm not one of your kids at the center."

"No, you're not. For one thing, my kids at the center can admit to themselves that it doesn't matter what they do, their parents will never love them the way they are. But you sit there and make garlic bread like a moron if you want to—he's still going to look at you like the last time you did anything right, you were eleven years old. You will never be what he wants."

It didn't matter how many times Maya apologized, or how much she'd cried when Eva came with Cheese to move the handful of things in the apartment that actually belonged to her. It didn't matter that Eva admitted, when pressed, that she'd been out of line bringing Maya's parents into it. There were moments when you knew things about what was inside of people you didn't want to, knew how deeply they could disappoint you. There was love, and then there was suicide—and then there was whatever it was she had with Cheese. A place to go whenever she needed it, but where she'd never feel good about being. They'd spent the night she left Maya, and most of the following morning, in bed together, until there was the sound of the phone ringing, and with a glance at the caller ID, Cheese took the call and headed into the living room with the phone. Eva had been ignoring the new girlfriend all morning, but the bedroom suddenly seemed full of things that belonged to her: a woman's belt, a paint-splattered T-shirt, a bottle of orange nail polish on the dresser. She turned the sound up on the television. On CNN, green bombs were falling somewhere, and Eva felt more chastened by the blurred night vision carnage than she had by the token reminders that another woman lived here now.

Cheese came back into the room a few minutes later. "Kate," he said. "She's upset about something. She was visiting her parents for the weekend, and I guess they had a fight. Eva—"

Eva exhaled. "If you're going to console distraught women all day, you're going to have to be more gentle about getting rid of them."

"Look, she won't be back tonight. But tomorrow—"

"So I can stay until the replacement gets here?"

"Eva—"

"No, fair is fair. But you might have at least been more original. Really, another artistic brown girl? It's like—"

"It's not like. It's not like anything."

"Right, she's a painter. And a different kind of brown. Watch, though, Arab is the new black."

"Now you're just being ridiculous."

Now? Eva thought. She could not remember the last time things had not been ridiculous.

"I'm sorry. I'll go."

She could have stayed, she knew that. She was Cheese's first Meaningful Girl, and she had left him. She could have stayed the night and been sitting there eating breakfast when the new girlfriend came back if she'd wanted to. When she'd left, she'd thought of it as a grand gesture toward Kate, the kind of supercilious magnanimity that was usually out of her reach. She came back again a week later. The silence of her sparse Washington Heights studio had been driving her crazy, and the noisy parade of life outside was no relief. She'd been expecting Cheese to awkwardly ask her to leave, or worse yet, to awkwardly invite her in and expect her to awkwardly socialize with Kate without letting on that anything had changed. Eva was surprised by the intensity of the relief she felt when Cheese told her Kate had gone to California for a few weeks *to think about their relationship*. She preferred not to focus on what it meant.

William wondered if there was a way to tell Eva how badly she needed him without insulting her. He worried that the best years of her life were going to look like the last few decades of his, that she'd be too proud to admit she needed him now, needed someone to let her put herself together, get a real job, go back to school maybe, find a decent boyfriend she could present in public, one who didn't leave her looking so disoriented all the time. While he was phrasing and rephrasing the invitation in his head, the waiter appeared with their food. He leaned over Eva a little too closely when putting her pasta in front of her, and gave her an overly friendly smile. *Watch it, that's my daughter,* William wanted to say, but he had never been able to say that about Eva. He didn't know what to protect her from, and anyway, she seemed to have taken her protection into her own hands some time ago.

He thought maybe he would show her a picture of the new place, though from the outside it didn't look like much. He'd been skeptical when the broker showed him the listing, not to mention skeptical of Brooklyn in general. As a child in the Bronx, he'd hated Brooklyn on principle—too much boasting on the part of its inhabitants, too low to the ground, too many trains involved in visiting anyone who lived there. But the apartment, the converted upper half of a Fort Greene brownstone, had won him over. There were two levels, and three bedrooms, and windows everywhere you looked. He had taken to walking around the neighborhood in the evenings. He ate roti one day and giant hamburgers the next. He was becoming a fan of Brooklyn's parks. He had once seen a young man in a T-shirt that read BROOKYLN. YOU KNOW BETTER. He wondered if this was the sort of person Eva would know.

The apartment had cost him the better portion of his savings, but it was a good investment, and good for him, after all these years of living a life he pretended he could leave at any minute, even as he got more and more settled, to own something, to put down roots. Besides, he had been making, for almost a decade, far more than he'd been spending, what with his ascetic lifestyle. He needed a place—and this was a good one, a place where they could rebuild things, a place where he could see Eva living, her art in one room, her in another, until she was on her feet, until whatever sad thing that surrounded her had been lifted.

"Listen," he said. "I've moved to Brooklyn. I got a real place to live. It's beautiful. Lots of room."

He did not mention the lack of furniture. He would get new furniture. He was fifty years old and he had never bought a piece of his own furniture. Even in the middle of the divorce, he had let Debra pick out what later sat in his old apartment for twenty years, and make arrangements for its delivery. This time he and Eva could find things they both liked, make sure she would be happy there. He'd thought of her in the big bedroom over the garden, sleeping safely, putting what she wanted on the walls. He'd remembered her racing through the small apartment he and Debra had shared so long ago, running down the hall with the light behind her. He'd remembered her stumbling into the kitchen sleepy-eyed on Sunday mornings, crawling into his lap and helping him grate cheese for the omelets Debra was making. He remembered what it was like to be at home in a place.

"Look," he said. "There's room for you. Two rooms. You must be so crowded in your studio. Your mother says there's not even

room for real furniture. You shouldn't be living that way. Come
with me. We'll get whatever you need. Stay as long as you need to
stay."

"Daddy," Eva said, pushing away the half-full plate of pasta. "Oh,
Daddy. That's wonderful for you, and wonderful for you to think
of me. But I think we'd just get in each other's way. Besides, I like
living in my studio, and you need your own space. Everybody needs
their own space."

Eva saw the look on her father's face and fought the urge to take
back what she'd said. He looked almost the way he had looked when
she and her mother had first left him. She closed her eyes and could
remember nothing but that morning years ago, dull sky, October
leaves on the ground. He had taken her to get a last slice of New
York pizza while her mother watched the moving men put the last of
their things on the truck.

"It's not so far away," he'd said. "Remember how much Daddy
loves you?"

"The whole world much and then some," she'd remembered.
She'd thought of love being like tentacles, reaching from wherever
he was to wherever she was. She'd giggled.

"Is that funny?" he'd asked.

"I am thinking of you like a jellyfish," she'd said, but he hadn't
understood.

Wherever You Go, There You Are

need you to take Chrissie for a little bit," Aunt Edie says, because apparently I pass for a role model these days. It's Thursday night, and they're standing on the doorstep, unannounced. Aunt Edie doesn't bother coming in. She looks exhausted, her eyes puffy from crying, her usually impeccably braided white hair hanging loose and disheveled. Her last living sibling, Chrissie's grandfather, has been in the hospital all summer, and odds are he isn't coming out again. I tell Aunt Edie that I'm going out of town tomorrow—which is true, there's a half-packed suitcase on my bed to prove it. She tells me I can take Chrissie with me, which more or less settles it. Chrissie breezes past me. Her footsteps on the creaking wood floor of my father's house swallow her hello. I have a long list of reasons why Chrissie shouldn't come on this trip, but few of them I'll admit to myself, let alone to my great-aunt. In any case, she isn't leaving much room for argument.

"I'm tired," says Aunt Edie. "She needs someone to look out for her, and I've got other things on my mind right now." She reaches into her purse and stretches out her hand to give me Chrissie's cell phone, which Chrissie is apparently banned from using. "Her father's not leaving Bobby's bedside," Aunt Edie goes on, "and Tia can't take her because she's too busy with nursing school, so that leaves you."

I stop myself from asking who it is Tia's supposed to be nursing. Tia is Aunt Edie's granddaughter, my cousin—Chrissie's, too— but she is not a nurse or a nursing student. She may possibly own a nursing uniform, but if she does, it has breakaway snaps and she's generally wearing a G-string under it. I don't know where Aunt Edie got nurse from, but no one's allowed to say Tia's a stripper. Tia's job bothers Aunt Edie for reasons involving hellfire and eternal damnation. It bothers me because even though Tia's twenty-five like I am, she looks thirteen. I love her, don't get me wrong, but she's got chicken legs, and nothing in the way of hips or boobs, and a big head with wide almond eyes and a long blond weave, and while I can imagine many reasons why men might pay good money to see a real live woman, there's something unsettling about so many of them paying to see a real live Bratz doll.

In fairness, there isn't much else to do in Waterton, Delaware. It's close to everything else in Delaware without actually being part of any of it—about an hour away from the noisy hedonism of Rehoboth Beach's and Ocean City's boardwalks, about an hour from the suburban sprawl subdivisions that might as well be North Maryland or South Jersey. It's not quite the Delaware that's mostly pig and tobacco farms, though there are farms in Waterton, and a fresh fruit and vegetable stand every mile or so, and the world's largest scrapple factory. When you approach the city limits from the highway, there's a painted wooden sign that says WELCOME TO WATERTON: WHEREVER YOU GO, THERE YOU ARE. It doesn't tell you that where you are is a city that gets seventy percent of its annual revenue from ticketing speeding tourists who got lost on their way to the beach. It's mostly a town that still exists because no one's gotten around to telling it that it can't anymore. The highlight of most people's weekends is losing money down at the Seahorse Casino, which is forty minutes away and not even a fun casino. It's just a big room full of slot machines and fluorescent light, and the only drinks they serve are shitty beer and something called Delaware Punch, which tastes less like punch and more like the Seahorse Casino is determined to single-handedly use up the nation's entire supply of banana schnapps. Considering the options, it makes sense that Tia does good business here.

I live here because right now I have no place else to be. The house I'm staying in is my father's, and was my grandfather's before that. It was either come here and be alone for a while, or move in with my mother, which would have felt like an admission of failure on both of our parts. The house is on the back corner of a parcel of land that was once large enough that it meant something for black people to own it back in the day, but it's been divided and subdivided through the years—split between children in wills, sold off piecemeal to developers, whittled down so that, between the fifteen of us, everyone in my generation probably owns about a square inch of it. My father moved into the house twenty years ago, after my parents' divorce, looking for a place to get his head together. Or at least, my father's furniture moved into the house; my father himself got into the antiques market and seems perpetually on a plane to some faraway place in pursuit of a stamp, a coin, a rare baseball card, anything of more-than-obvious value.

Now that I'm here again, I can hardly blame him for leaving so often; I am learning the hard way that it's not a good place to get over anything. In every room of the house, fighting with my father's coin chests and signed sports posters and ceramic knickknacks, there's a reminder of what people are supposed to mean to each other. The set of initials carved into the handmade frame of the front door. A sepia-toned photograph of my grandparents, who died within weeks of each other, months after their forty-fifth anniversary. The lavender corsage my grandmother wore at her wedding; my uncle Bobby found it pressed into my grandfather's Bible decades later and had it framed on the wall of the master bedroom. The wooden archway leading to the dining room, the one that had been knocked down and rebuilt by my father at Uncle Bobby's request, the year a foot amputation confined his late wife to a wheelchair too big to fit through the original doorway. The wedding quilt on the living room wall, the one thing besides their life savings that my grandparents had salvaged from the house they fled in Georgia, hours before a mob torched it on a trumped-up theft charge. As a child, I'd taken comfort in the house's memorabilia—I imagined this was the sort of unconditional love that all adults had eventually—but now, fresh off the end of my last relationship, the house feels like a museum of lack: here is the sort of love you never saw up close, here are souvenirs from all the places your father was when he was not with you, here is something whole that one day you will own a fraction of.

Chrissie's sprawled out on the bed I've been sleeping in since I got here a few months ago. It's the same bed I slept in when I visited here as a kid, with the same Strawberry Shortcake sheets I never had the heart to tell my father I outgrew, and lying on them Chrissie looks like a little kid herself. Her hair is tied up in a silk headscarf, which means she must have spent half a day blow-drying and flat-ironing it movie-star straight, humidity be damned. She's wearing cut-offs and ratty sneakers and smells like a bottle of tamarind perfume I remember her borrowing from me the last time she was over here.

Chrissie's parents are splitting and she's spending the summer in Waterton, Delaware, with her father because that's supposed to make her OK with it, except her father's been cocooning himself in the hospital all summer, and Chrissie's spent most of her time so far playing hearts with Aunt Edie and the two widows next door, and the rest of it mysteriously unaccounted for, though Tia's filled me in on some rumors.

"Where are you going?" Chrissie asks me, nudging my suitcase with her elbow.

"We're going to North Carolina, I guess. Aunt Edie wants you to come with me."

"What's in North Carolina?"

I consider the question. "A friend" would be a lie of omission; "an ex" would put Brian in the same category as Jay, who I came here to get away from. Jay, who still lives in the apartment with my name on the lease and is probably fucking another girl on my sofa right now. Jay, who earlier this week sent me an e-mail that seemed to presume

I would take time off from not speaking to him, and working on my own dissertation ("She Real Cool: The Art and Activism of Gwendolyn Brooks"), in order to proofread his ("Retroactive Intentionality: [Re]Reading Radical Artists' Self-Assessments").

"A friend," I say. "Brian. He's in a band. He wants me to see his show."

"A friend you're meeting in your underwear?" Chrissie asks, sitting up and gesturing toward my suitcase, which for the time being contains nothing but toiletries and underwear. She arches her eyebrows at me and giggles. "What kind of show does he want you to see?"

"I haven't thought about the clothes yet. Underwear is the easy part of packing. There's no deciding. You can't go wrong with underwear."

"So the only panties you own are black lace?" she asks, smirking into the suitcase.

"Shut up," I say. "You shouldn't be looking through other people's underwear. And what do you know about lace underwear, anyway?"

Chrissie blushes so red I'm sorry I asked, and then just as quickly starts singing, "*I see London, I see France, Brian's gonna see Carla's slutty underpants . . .*"

Given my history with Brian, this is too close to true. Every item of non-underwear clothing I've considered packing I've rejected because it would seem like a deliberate provocation. I don't own much that Brian hasn't ripped off of me at some point in the past, even when he was seeing other women, even when he was with the fiancée before the one I'm ostensibly going down there to meet. I shush Chrissie off to bed while I finish packing, but I hear her in the next room, tossing and turning, riffling through the pages of a magazine. When I finally zip my suitcase shut, I go back into the bedroom to check on her. I haven't seen too much of Chrissie since I've been in town, and she thinks I've been avoiding her. She's probably right: lately watching Chrissie has been like watching a taped recording of my own adolescence, which is nothing I want to revisit.

Though the lights are off in the bedroom when I go to check on her, I can tell Chrissie's only pretending to be asleep.

"Night, Chris," I say.

"Night," she mumbles.

"Hey," she calls as I start to leave. "Can Tia come with us tomorrow? It'd be fun. Like a girls' road trip."

I consider the many reasons why this would not be fun. Tia never liked Brian. Once he made the mistake of telling her he understood oppression because he was half Irish and one-eighth Native American. After that, Tia always called him he-who-has-metal-in-his-face, because of his eyebrow piercing. Brian never liked Tia, except for that one time in college he drunkenly asked me if I thought she'd be into a threesome, and I stopped speaking to him for a month.

"Tia's working," I say. "And anyway, she needs to be around in case anything happens with Uncle Bobby. Aunt Edie's going to need her."

"People are going to need us too," Chrissie protests. "He's my grandfather."

"Of course they will," I say. "We'll come back if anything happens."

The truth is, I'm not sure who needs me. My father paid an obligatory visit to Uncle Bobby, and then did what he does: he's spending the summer in India looking at death statues. We are all walking around on eggshells, waiting for a death the way people wait on rainstorms when the sky promises bad weather, but so far nobody has talked to me about it, and nobody has asked me to do anything more difficult than make potato salad.

It's afternoon by the time we get on the road the next day, and we spend hours stuck in beach traffic. Chrissie's awake enough to resent that I've confined her cell phone to the glove compartment. It's beeping because someone's left her a message, and between the beeping and her whining, I'm thinking of opening the glove compartment myself. My cigarettes are in there, but nobody, especially Chrissie, is supposed to know I smoke when I'm stressed.

"It could be my parents," she says. I ignore this.

"We might as well not even be driving," Chrissie says. "And I'm hungry."

"Well, then you should have eaten when we stopped for brunch," I say. Chrissie has been doing this thing where whenever we eat out together, she orders whatever I order, then suddenly remembers she can't eat it because she's on a diet, and has two bites and three glasses of water instead. At the diner on the way out of town, she had three french fries and a mouse-sized nibble of her grilled cheese.

"I wasn't hungry when we stopped," she says.

"Then you can wait until we get to Richmond for dinner."

The traffic picks up around the Bay Bridge. In the glove compartment Chrissie's phone is still beeping something insistent.

"You should let me get it," she says. "What if my grandfather died?"

"Then someone would have called me," I say.

Both pleas for her phone having failed, Chrissie sulks, actively. Her sulking takes the form of rummaging through her miniature beaded purse in search of beauty product after beauty product. When she is done with the glitter lotion and the lip gloss and the eye shadow, it's true her skin has a glow to it, but her hands are covered in sparkles, like a kid who's just finished an art project.

"I'll let you answer the phone when you tell me why Aunt Edie doesn't want you to have it in the first place," I say.

"I've got a boyfriend," Chrissie says.

"Of course you do," I say.

"So, I can talk to him?"

"Pick up the phone if you want, but you shouldn't, he's an asshole."

"You've never even seen him."

"Don't have to," I say. "He's a fifteen-year-old boy, which means he's an asshole by default, or he's older than that, in which case he's an asshole for dating you."

"I don't look fourteen," says Chrissie, which answers one question but isn't any kind of counterargument to my original point. It's true, though, she doesn't look fourteen, in the way no girl looks fourteen once she's got tits and an ass like Chrissie's and men have stopped looking at her face. She's the wrong kind of pretty, the kind that's soft but not fragile, the kind that inspires the impulse to touch.

. . .

The boyfriend doesn't answer when Chrissie calls him back.

"*Asshole,*" she mutters.

"Look at the water," I say, because we're driving over the Chesapeake, and I've always thought it was a beautiful view, the wires of the bridge cutting into the image of the water beneath. Passing through the bridge with the sloping wires on either side always feels to me like being inside of a giant stringed instrument. Chrissie looks sideways out the window for a second, then turns back to me.

"We're going all the way to North Carolina just to see this guy?" she asks.

"What else do you want to do?"

"I think maybe I should go to a doctor."

"What's wrong with you?" I ask. I'm already checking out the traffic headed back to Delaware, because if this kid tells me she's pregnant I'm turning the car around and giving her back to Aunt Edie. I've already done my lifetime share of abortion hand-holding.

"I think my vagina's broken," she says.

"OK," I say. "OK, look. I don't know what that means, and I don't think I want to, because as far as I'm concerned, you don't have a vagina and won't for ten years, and even then I probably won't want to hear much about it, OK? Talk to your mother about this stuff."

"If I ever met a woman without a vagina, it's my mother," Chrissie says.

"Don't say that," I say, because you're supposed to remind people how they actually do love their parents. Chrissie's mom is away at a summerlong church retreat. For a while she sent Chrissie post-cards that said things like YOU'RE NEVER ALONE WHEN YOU'RE WITH JESUS and I PUT ALL OF MY EGGS IN ONE BASKET AND GAVE THEM TO THE LORD. Chrissie finally wrote back, *Can Jesus make me an omelet, then? He's kind of a crappy mom otherwise.* She hasn't gotten a post-card since.

"Is something wrong?" I ask. "Are you sick or something?"

"No," she says, "but we tried to have sex last week and I hadn't done it before and it didn't work."

"What do you mean, 'it didn't work'?"

"It wouldn't go in," she says. "So he stopped and I left because I thought maybe there was something wrong with me."

"Well, what did you do beforehand?" I ask.

When she answers, it becomes clear to me that this kid has no idea what's supposed to be happening, and neither does her boyfriend. I feel kind of sorry for her entire generation, because they've learned all the theatrical parts of sex so they walk around pouting and posing like little baby porn stars, and all the clinical parts of sex so they know when to demand penicillin, but not the basic mechanical processes of actual pleasure, which everyone assumes someone else has covered. I didn't know shit about sex when I was her age, but at least I was allowed to say so; no one expected us to be certified experts. It's not my subject of choice, but I don't know who else will explain things to her, except maybe Tia, which seems dangerous. When I'm done, I tack on a speech about how she's fourteen and emotional right now and he's probably too old for her and even if there's a condom it could break or fall off and she could die, and besides, she's not comfortable enough with her body to enjoy anything that happens to it yet, and there's lots of things she can do that aren't actually fucking.

Maybe I've kind of freaked her out, because somewhere north of Columbia we pass a Friendly's, and she gets all excited about it. Even though we're nowhere near Richmond I agree to stop when she asks. She's dropped the diet stuff, at least, but if you've ever seen anything more disturbing than a kid eating a Reese's Pieces Happy Face Sundae after you've just explained to her how to give a proper blow job, I don't want to hear about it.

Chrissie sleeps most of the rest of the way to Raleigh. I could use her to keep an eye on the map, because I've only been down here a handful of times, and I hate this stretch of highway. There's something about the compressed space of cars that makes people want to say things out loud, maybe just to see what echoes back, and every memory I have of this part of 95 is a memory of argument. The first time I went to Raleigh, I was about Chrissie's age and my mom was driving. On the way back, we were trying to get out of the state a few hours ahead of the tropical storm that was on its way, but already it was thundering and lightning, and the rain was steadily splattering onto our windshield, distorting everything on the other side faster than the windshield wipers could clear it.

The argument we'd been having was stupid. It was Father's Day, and she wanted me to call her boyfriend, this jackass dentist she'd been seeing for a while, and wish him a happy Father's Day. The dentist was always blowing my mother off at the last minute. He yelled when they fought, and sulked when he didn't get his way. He'd stretched his fairly substantial income to its natural limits, and was always "borrowing" money from my mom that we never got back. You could smell the bullshit coming off of him, unless you were my mother, and then you thought he was the answer to our prayers. I said the dentist had his own kids and I already had a father to call, and my mother said my father was out of the country and the dentist's kids weren't going to call him, and I said that's because even they know he's an asshole. My mother got all huffy and cried and said she was just trying to have a family, and I said she already had a family, at least until I was eighteen and I could get away from her crazy ass, and she pulled over and slapped me and then said, *I'm getting out now*, and until the car door opened and the sting of the rain hit me, I didn't know out of what.

Through the stream of rain on the windshield, I watched my mother get smaller and smaller because of distance and water. It was like watching a person deflate. I understood that if she wasn't coming back, I wasn't going anywhere, not because I was still a few months away from my learner's permit, but because I lacked the instinct to run. I understood, for the first time, how much I loved my mother. I understood that if I could help it, I would never love anybody that much again. When she got back in the car ten minutes later, soaking wet and both of us still crying, we didn't say a word about it—not then, not all the way back to DC.

I want to wake Chrissie and tell her about this as if it's a warning: Don't push too hard; your last chance to see a person the way you wanted them to be may come at any moment. One minute you have a parent, or a friend, or a lover, something solid, and physics tells you their resistance will always be there to meet you as you press yourself into relief against them. Then all of a sudden your mother is a fading outline in a thunderstorm, wet and weak and so far out of reach; or your lover who may also be your best and only friend is pulled so quickly into someone else's life that you don't even realize he's left yours until you're getting a save-the-date card; or your father is somewhere at the other end of the world and even if you had a number for him, you'd feel wrong calling to tell him to quit collecting stuff when it's painfully clear that you have nothing to offer to replace it. But I don't wake Chrissie because she's sleeping like a baby, and anyway, she isn't a baby and she doesn't need me to tell her what it is to watch somebody let you down by being human in the saddest and neediest ways, what it is to push at something that has long since given way. It hits me like my mother's slap that just watching me these days is teaching her this lesson.

I wake Chrissie up just before the highway exit so she can read me the rest of the directions. The bar is not hard to find and has its own parking lot. On the outside it's kind of like a giant cottage, mute stucco with a brown shingled roof. Inside, it's big and dimly lit. The ceilings are high and the splintered wooden rafters are showing. We're still early for the show and there are only a handful of people in the bar. I can see Brian onstage with his back to me. I try to sneak up on him, but before I get all the way there he turns around.

"Hey, stranger," he says, hopping down from the stage. He hugs me like I've just gotten back from a war. The smell of him is like if someone made a perfume out of cigarette smoke. "I missed you, kid."

"I missed you too," I say, kissing him on the cheek. Chrissie smirks beside me, and starts humming the underpants song under her breath again.

"Who's this?" asks Brian, taking note of Chrissie for the first time.

"I gotta pee," says Chrissie. She walks off in the other direction. The sound of her heels against the floor of the mostly empty bar is less of a controlled staccato and more of a *stomp, stomp, stomp*.

"Who was *that*?" asks a shaggy-looking guy messing with the keyboard.

"*That's* fourteen and it's my cousin," I say. "I've got a knife in my pocketbook and I will cut you if you touch her."

"Shame," says the keyboardist. "You legal, then?"

"Stop flirting with my sister," says Brian, hugging me to him again.

Brian and I call each other brother and sister because it lets us pretend we have an excuse for still knowing each other. In anyone else's life, Brian would be the college ex I never spoke to again, and I would be the crazy ex who'd once deliberately destroyed his brand-new guitar. But instead of being embarrassed by everything that's happened between us, we're both comforted by the fact that someone else has seen us at all of our possible worsts and hung around anyway.

There was a point, maybe even a year, where we were fucking each other for the conversation afterward. Not that the sex was bad, it just wasn't the point anymore. We talked about our futures, the ones we never dared to imagine being full of anything but chaos. We toasted to the shortcomings of the various potential stepparents we'd grown up with: between the two of us, nineteen in total. When he was at his drunkest, he always told me the story about the time his mother passed him off as a neighbor she babysat, in order to date a banker who didn't want kids, and when we were done laughing as though it were hysterical, him imitating the banker and his eight-year-old self, one of us would cry for real, and I would hold him and tell him I was sorry he was so fucked up, and he would tell me he was sorry I was fucked up enough to want him anyway.

"So, where's this poor girl you've tricked into marrying you?" I ask. "Is she locked up somewhere so she doesn't escape before the wedding?"

"Ha," says Brian, but his smile feels forced. "She's on her way. Alan and I came in the van with the equipment."

The last time Brian got engaged, he would have cracked up at the joke. The last girl was an actress, someone he met at an Exxon convenience store on a road trip right after the play she was in had ended its run. They'd gotten engaged a month later, two weeks before she got called to New York for a better gig. Brian came to see me right after she left, and we'd spent the weekend in bed with each other, him talking about how wonderful she was, me reminding him of all the other women he'd said that about. I'd met Jay two weeks later. When Brian's engagement inevitably fell through, we joked that if things had ended between them a few months sooner, he could have kept the wedding date and married me instead.

Brian and I almost did get married once, but not for real for real.

We were in Vegas, which is a city I've always loved for its ability to be at once shameless about its fantasy self and honest about its real one, which is the only reason I've ever loved anything. A college friend with too much money had invited us out there for a birthday party, and we were champagne-drunk and tired of the Strip one night. I said I'd always wanted to get married in Vegas, because marriage was just a big flashy spectacle designed to cover up the tacky tragedy of human loneliness, and why would you get married anywhere you could forget that? Brian said he'd always wanted Elvis at his wedding, but only if it was fat Elvis, and anyway, us being us we might as well get our first divorces out of the way early. All of it was kind of a joke and kind of not, and I don't remember why we didn't do it, just that we ended up riding those gondola boats around the underground of The Venetian all night instead.

Brian bounces off to get me a vodka tonic, extra lime—he doesn't have to ask what I'm drinking—and while I'm waiting for him to come back, or Chrissie to reappear from the ladies' room, the fiancée walks in the front door. I haven't seen her picture, but I know her right away. She's wearing a vintage Wonder Woman T-shirt stretched tight across her chest, and Brian's got a thing for both boobs and comic books. She's cute. Platinum blond hair, layered and flipped up at the ends, a dab of frosted lip gloss. If her look was a smell, it would be grape bubble gum. Her name is Miranda. Brian met her at the go-kart track two years ago, but they've only been dating six months. She's an elementary school teacher who moonlights as a semiprofessional local comedian. Ever since he met her, I get random text messages from him, jokes and one-liners, and I know it means he's watching her perform.

She obviously recognizes me when she sees me, and even though her smile seems genuine, I resent this girl already—not for having him, but because I'll have to have her now. She's like a crayon drawing he's handing me, and like her or not I'll have to pin her to my refrigerator for years.

"So, what do you think?" Brian whispers when he returns with my drink.

"Nicely done," I say.

He looks relieved. When Miranda comes over, she hugs me first, awkwardly smushing into the hand I'd extended to shake hers.

"I'm sorry," she says, laughing a little as she pulls away. "Was that weird? I feel like we already know each other."

"No," I lie. I'm saved from making further small talk when Chrissie finally rejoins us, looking like she's ready for a glamour shot. She's let her hair down and combed some sort of glitter through it, and put on mounds of blush and eye shadow and a coffee-colored lipstick that's a good two shades too dark for her skin tone. I can't open my mouth to tell her to wash her face, because I'm too busy trying not to laugh at her.

"Your sister?" Miranda asks.

"Cousin," I say.

"Clearly, good looks run in the family," she says. Her voice flutters a little when she laughs. "And those are great shoes," she says to Chrissie.

It's as if she has studied a playbook on meeting your fiancé's ex-girlfriend. Chrissie looks at me like she doesn't know whether it's OK to accept the compliment. I look away, because I don't want her to think she needs my permission to like the girl, but I also don't want to give it. Besides, Chrissie's shoes are tacky stiletto sandals from Payless, and I probably should have talked her out of them this morning.

Brian ushers Miranda and me to a table up front, and then disappears to bring back drinks for her and Chrissie. By the time he gets back, a beer for her and a Shirley Temple for Chrissie, a decent crowd has started to filter in. Before the set he squeezes my hand for luck, then gives Miranda a closed-mouth kiss. Chrissie watches this like it's a spectator sport, and seems pleased enough that I've brought her into my real life that she's reconciled herself with the indignity of drinking the Shirley Temple.

"This is kind of all right," she says when Brian finally starts playing, which, given her usual tone these days, is like she's handing him a Grammy.

Watching Brian perform always makes me feel weirdly proprietary about him, which is stupid, because this is the thing about him that *has* to be public. But I was there when he was making this shit up on his guitar, and when he'd wake up at three a.m. to whisper a song into my ear, and when he was ready to give it all up and get a real job and I told him not to. When Miranda leans forward into the music and closes her eyes like Brian is singing to her directly, something in me snaps. "Isn't he great?" she whispers to me between songs, opening her eyes again and looking so sincere that I have to look away to stop myself from telling her he isn't really hers, that she only loves him because she'll never know him the way I do. It makes me happy when I recognize myself in a lyric, even if the lyric is *I lied, you lied, I lied, to really love something is suicide*, because how I feel about Brian hasn't been about love in a long time, it's been about mattering the most, and as I count the songs, I'm confident I'm still winning on that scorecard.

When the set is over, Brian and the keyboardist, Alan, disappear backstage for a minute, and Miranda asks a million questions about Delaware. I let Chrissie answer most of them, which means that the answer she gets most frequently is "dumb," followed closely by "stupid."

"Still," says Miranda, "summer's great when you're a kid, isn't it? I get jealous of my students sometimes—they don't know how good they have it."

"Summer's awesome," says Chrissie. "My grandfather's dying. And my dad won't even talk to me about it, and my parents just got divorced, and my mom's at Bible camp trying to join some weirdo cult thing because she's lonely and is trying to pretend Jesus is her boyfriend, and *my* boyfriend works at a gas station and has never left the state of Delaware, even though he's older than me and Delaware is, like, ten feet big and he apparently doesn't understand enough about sex to make it work right so I can fuck him to get my mind off things."

She takes an emphatic sip of her Shirley Temple, even though the drink is nothing but melting red ice by now, and stomps back to the bathroom. A guy at the bar reaches for her arm as she passes him, but she doesn't break stride long enough to notice.

. . .

"I'm sorry," Miranda says, sliding her chair out of the way so I can go after Chrissie. I stay put.

"She'll be fine," I say, by which I mean that I can't help her. I think of offering to get Miranda a drink, but her first beer is still barely half gone, an observation that prompts me to push my own empty glass behind a napkin holder. The tables in the bar are covered in old newsprint that's been lacquered over, and I try to make out the words to one of the stories shellacked beneath my drink, but can't read it in the dim light. Beside it, a vintage ad warns me: *Perspiration Ruins Panty Hose!*

"Is this weird for you?" Miranda finally asks.

"Which part?" I ask, and she doesn't press it. I keep an eye on the bathroom door to see when Chrissie comes out.

"I know about all the nonsense, with him and women," she says after a minute. "I'm not an idiot. I'm not pretending this is foolproof. But you should see how serious he is about things these days. About his music. About not fucking up the way he has before. About being honest with himself. About dealing with all the stuff he's not over. You made him a better person. I hope you know that."

"If I did," I say, "it was an accident."

I laugh, and we both pretend I'm kidding.

By the time Brian and the keyboardist stop mingling with the crowd and selling ten-dollar CDs with homemade covers, Chrissie and her slightly smudged mascara have rejoined us. Miranda and Chrissie and I are doing our best impressions of people having fun in a bar, and I find it briefly hysterical the work we're putting into emotionally containing ourselves in front of a guy who prints out all of his song lyrics and sets them on fire in mini trash cans when he gets really angry, until it occurs to me that maybe he doesn't do that anymore. While a folksinger in a long tie-dye dress sets up her sound equipment, the speaker continues playing the crappy Top Forty that started when Brian went off, and Alan grimaces. He's taken off the black collared shirt he performed in and is wearing a T-shirt that says I'M NOT A GYNECOLOGIST, BUT I'LL TAKE A LOOK. His arms beneath the cap sleeves are covered in baby-fine hairs, dirty blond like the hair on his head. *Dirty* is the right adjective for him altogether. Chrissie whispers something into his ear that I hope is music-related, but probably isn't because of the way he turns away from her and licks his upper lip. He whispers something back to her and she smiles.

"Alan," says Miranda, while I'm still trying to figure out where to intervene, but he ignores her and keeps talking to Chrissie.

"There's your smile," he says. "Not that you don't have great pouting lips, but something's gotta give. You're fourteen, right? Whatever it is, it's not forever."

"My parents are splitting," she says again. "And my grandfather is dying. So it's pretty much forever." She does this dramatic half-sigh thing and puts her pout back on.

"Chrissie," I say, "stop it."

It's not that I doubt she's upset, it's that I'm watching her turn into the kind of girl who always needs to assert that something tangible is wrong in order to justify making things worse. Alan knows she's overdoing it, too, because he smirks a little and raises his beer glass.

"To death and divorce, then," he says, "which are forever."

"And marriage," I say, clinking my drink to his and nodding at Brian, "which is not."

Miranda's looking at Brian like she's waiting for him to say something, and he's looking at the floor like the universe will work this one out without him. I look at Miranda, the startled flicker in her eyes fading to something almost wounded as Brian stays silent, and for a second I feel something like triumph. Then I look at Chrissie. Her pout is gone, and she is smiling at me with a giddy sort of pride. It makes me want to hit something that this is the thing that has finally put me entirely back in her good graces.

Miranda grabs her purse from the back of the chair, and makes a show of fishing out her keys. When she finds them, she holds them aloft for a second, like she's not sure what happens next.

"OK," she says, standing up. Nobody looks at her directly. "I'm going home."

"I'm sorry," I say. "It was just a joke. I shouldn't have said it."

"I hope next time we meet, you find our engagement just slightly less hysterical," she says. "I want to like you. Brian wants me to like you."

Brian still doesn't look up. "Are you coming with me?" Miranda asks. He throws up his arms as if this decision is out of his hands.

"I can't leave before Angie's set is over," Brian says. "I'll call you later. I'll get a ride home with Alan."

"Yeah you will," says Miranda, and I want to tell her right then how much I like her, how at this point the last fiancée would have been weeping and begging and making a total fool of herself, but she's already leaving. Brian doesn't get up.

"You're a bitch," Brian says to me—not like he's mad, just like it's an observation.

I turn to Chrissie to tell her to go outside for a second, but Alan is already motioning her toward the bar. I let them go and turn back to Brian.

"I'm sorry," I say. "This probably wasn't the best week for this. We're all a little high-strung."

"Are you OK?" he asks. He puts a hand on my knee. There's a faint flicker of a scar below his index finger, from where I accidentally burned him with a cigarette lighter once.

"I'm as OK as I get."

"I really do love her," he says. "Not the idea of her, but her. This isn't like the other times. I'm trying to do something right here."

"Which other times?" I ask.

"Don't do that," he says. "I'm not going to lie to you about what you and I were. Are."

"I know," I say. "I know. I'll apologize to her tomorrow."

"If she's speaking to me tomorrow," he says.

"Why wouldn't she be?"

"Right," he says. His hand is still on my knee. "Why wouldn't she be? I'll call her later."

I lean into him and reach for the cigarettes in his shirt pocket, and brush my arm against his while he lights my cigarette.

"I should get Chrissie," I say, but I don't look away from him. The look in his eyes could melt glass.

Chrissie's laughter from across the room interrupts our silent negotiation. She's standing at the bar with Alan and a girl in a tissue-thin tank top. Alan's already got his hand on Tank Top Girl's hip, and Chrissie's holding something in her hand that is clearly not a Shirley Temple and probably not straight soda. Her eyes are scanning the room, and I assume she's looking not for me but for a guy she can use to make Alan jealous, because she doesn't realize she's already lost this fight.

"I should get her out of here," I say. "Where'd you find that asshole?"

"Please," says Brian. "If I weren't here and you weren't babysitting, you'd have gone home with him already."

"I go home with a lot of assholes," I say. "At least I don't love any of them anymore."

"Really?" says Brian.

"I'm over Jay," I say. "We don't speak. And anyway, he told me once that love was not a real thing because it was *comprised of too many subsidiary emotions*."

I wait for Brian to laugh, but he doesn't.

"Jay wasn't the one I was talking about," he says finally.

"Stop," I say. I look away from him and then turn back.

Brian told me once that I was the only woman in the world he was completely honest with. He said my problem with relationships is that I make everyone feel like it's good enough to be who they actually are. At the time I had thought these were both good things.

"Trust me on this," he'd said. "Appreciate the liars. When people don't hide things, it means they don't care enough to be afraid of losing you."

Chrissie finally seems to realize she's been outplayed and starts to head back to the table. Behind her, Alan has his hand on the small of Tank Top Girl's back and is leaning in to her ear. I watch Chrissie walk to us. I can tell her heels have started to hurt her, because she's scooting her feet across the floor instead of picking them up all the way. As she gets closer, I slide away from Brian. Chrissie stops halfway between the bar and our table and looks over her shoulder to see if Alan's even noticed she's gone. She's smart enough to look only a little disappointed when she sees he's still thoroughly engrossed in Tank Top Girl's earlobe. When she sits back down at the table, I slide her half-full drink away from her.

"Hey," she says, "I'm thirsty."

"You should've thought about that before you asked Alan to put rum in your drink."

"You should have thought about that before you brought me to a bar."

"Touché," I say. "We're leaving soon."

Chrissie looks curiously at Brian, then glances back at me, and I try to relax my face into blank nonchalance, as if she's the only one immature enough to imagine this night ending differently.

It's barely after midnight when I finish my cigarette and Chrissie's drink, and Chrissie pretends she wants to stay through the end of the folksinger. It's the worst pretext ever: the folksinger is singing a song that's about either a blow job or her psych medication, and she keeps wailing, *You cannot make me swallow,* and no one wants to listen to that. I'm hugging Brian good-bye and apologizing again when the phone rings. It's Tia. I step outside because I can't hear her over the background noise.

"Where the fuck are you?" she says.

"I'm in North Carolina," I say, "with Chrissie. I told you we were going."

"Did you?" she says. "Well, look, get back here. Uncle Bobby died. Everyone's at the hospital."

"OK," I say, and I take a minute to go get Chrissie, not because I'm broken up, but because I feel like I'm supposed to be and I can't walk back in there too composed.

When I tell Chrissie, she doesn't lose it at first. We're standing outside the bar, and then she sits on the toadstool bench outside the place with her arms folded across her chest and the overhead light washing out her makeup. She looks like such a little kid then that I'm sorry I brought her here to begin with. For a minute she doesn't say anything, and then the floodgates open. It's the first time I've actually seen her cry in years, and it's so much that crying isn't even the right word for it. Brian comes out to check on us but when he sees her he walks to the corner of the parking lot.

"He doesn't even fucking talk to me," Chrissie says, when she can talk again. "All summer I've been there, and he doesn't even fucking talk to me. I would have sat there with him. I would have sat in that hospital with him all fucking summer long."

"He's trying to be a good dad," I say. "He's trying to protect you. He's trying to be a man about things."

"Yeah, well. He's being an asshole," she says.

"They don't really know the difference," I say. "You'll go home. He'll feel better. He won't say it, but he will."

"*I* won't feel better," she says, "I won't ever feel better."

"You will," I say, which may be a lie.

The best thing about the two years I spent with Jay is that splitting the rent let me pay off my credit cards, so I'm able to put Chrissie on a last-minute red-eye flight to Baltimore. Tia promises to pick her up there when the flight lands. I don't go back with her because of the car and because there's nothing for me to do there yet. The next few days will be comfort and shifting obligations, but no one will miss me or need me the way Chrissie's father needs her right now. My own will take a few days to fly back from India, and his current girlfriend, someone he met on a cruise to London, will be with him to comfort him in the meantime. Aunt Edie will have Tia. I am, for a moment, absurdly jealous of Chrissie, because there is not a single person in the world my mere presence will comfort right now, not a single place I need to be more than this one.

Brian's waiting in my car outside the airport. He drives without asking me which hotel, and I know if I end up at his apartment I'm not sleeping on the couch, but the thought of waking up next to him suddenly feels more terrifying than comforting, more like undoing something than fixing it.

"Stop," I say. "Stop the car."

"We're on the highway," he says.

"So get off the fucking highway, then," I say. At first I think he's going to ignore me, but he gets off at the next exit and pulls into the parking lot of a Waffle House just past the exit ramp.

"What's wrong now?" he asks.

I don't answer him, I just get out of the car and slam the door. It's still Saturday night in the parking lot—more drunk strangers and other people's problems than I can handle right now—so, after watching a girl vomit into the bushes and then go back to screaming at someone on her cell phone, I bang on the window until Brian leans over and opens the passenger-side door. I sit back in the seat and fasten my seat belt while he leans his forehead against the steering wheel. If I didn't know him better, I might think he was praying. I turn away from him and look out the windshield, into the window of the Waffle House in front of us.

If you have ever been to a pancake house in the middle of the night, then you know how resolutely depressing it is—you live in one of the few cities where it is never actually the middle of the night. In a city like this one, the first hour or so after bar time may be upbeat, because people are still trying to get something from the night: joy or sex or gradual sobriety. At around five a.m. you'll see the first waves of people beginning the new day or ending the night with sleepless exuberance. But between those hours, the pancake house is a dead zone for possibility. Everyone is there for lack of something: good and nourishing food, sufficient coordination to drive the rest of the way home, an appropriate person to love or fuck, a reason to get up the next morning.

I allow myself to say out loud that maybe it is simple lack, and not some unbreakable connection, that has kept Brian and me attached to each other all this time; that for a long time all I've been in his presence is the absence of better things. He stays quiet. Through the window, I watch a middle-aged man in a trucker hat stare at the back silhouette of a girl in ripped fishnets and a too-tight miniskirt, not exactly lecherously, but like she is a planet he has never been to, something so far out of this reality that he might as well look carefully.

"Just fucking go," I say to Brian. "I'll be fine if you just go."

I can hear him breathing, and his arm is touching mine, but just barely.

"This is me," he says. "I'm not going to leave you. And anyway, it's your goddamn car, and I'm not walking home."

"Fine, then. Stay," I say.

I look away from the Waffle House window and back toward the highway. The traffic keeps going by, candy-painted SUVs, slick sports cars, an eighteen-wheeler.

"I should take you to your hotel," Brian says quietly, but he doesn't start the engine and he doesn't get out of the car, and we sit there like that, waiting for something better to present itself.

Robert E. Lee Is Dead

For making honor roll you got these stupid Mylar balloons. They were silver on the back and red or blue or pink on the front, with CONGRATULATIONS written in big clashing letters. The balloons were supplied by the army recruiters who had an office across the street from our football field, and they always stuck a green and white U.S. Army sticker on the back. If you lived in Lakewood, then when you got a balloon your parents picked you up, or you drove yourself home with it in the backseat. Either way, when you got it home, you waited for your balloon to deflate slowly; and when it finally did, your mother smoothed out the wrinkles and put it on a wall, or in an album, or in a storage box somewhere, if you already had so many that another would be redundant. If you lived in Eastdale, then the stupid balloon got in your way the whole time you were walking home.

Geena Johnson and I lived in Eastdale. I knew her name already—everybody did—but Geena was a girl like sunlight: if you were a girl like I was back then, you didn't look at her directly. Usually there were girls following Geena's lead, often literally, wobbling behind her in platform boots they had just barely learned to walk in, but she was alone the first day she actually spoke to me. From the top of the hill where our high school began, I had seen her walking ahead of me, briskly and by herself. When she got to the chain-link fence encircling the water dam at the bottom of the hill, Geena threw her backpack over the top of the fence, balanced the heel of her boot against its wobbly surface, and expertly hoisted herself over, barely breaking stride. When I hopped the fence a few moments later, I took my time. Even in sneakers I was not as slick as Geena, and plus, the balloon kept hitting the side of my face and trying to pop itself on the top of the fence. I was less awkward crossing the high, rickety bridge that was probably the reason the water dam shortcut was closed off to begin with. I took some perverse pleasure in knowing that a fall at the right angle could have killed me, one slip, and no more Crystal.

On the other side of the dam, home surprised me. I always took a minute to recognize my own neighborhood. It seemed like every day a new apartment building was being built or an older store or house torn down. Things changed quickly in those years: Eastdale pushed into the suburb of Lakewood from one side, while white flight created suburbs of the suburbs on the other. This was the *new* New South: same rules, new languages. The people who could afford to leave Lakewood left; the ones who couldn't put up better fences. The rest of us were left in Eastdale: old houses, garden apartments, signs in Spanish and Vietnamese. We adapted well enough; we could all curse in Spanish and we'd skip school for noodle soup as soon as we'd skip for McDonald's. The handful of white kids who still lived in Eastdale adopted linguistic affectations with varying degrees of success and would have nothing to do with the Lakewood kids. Eastdale kids and Lakewood kids walked on opposite sides of the hallway and ate on opposite sides of the cafeteria and probably would have worn opposite-colored clothes if they could have coordinated it without communicating. The neighborhood in the immediate vicinity of our high school was called The Crossroads; don't ever let anyone tell you that the South is big on subtlety.

Geena and I weren't big on subtlety, either—not then, anyway. We were fourteen; she was flashy, I was brave the way you are when you don't know what you have to lose. When I emerged on the other side of the dam and walked the wrong way down the side of the parkway just because I could, I was not surprised to see her ahead of me, doing the same. My balloon mirrored our walk in a hazy silver film: ELENA'SCHICKENARROZCONPOLLO29.99MANICUREANDPEDICURE PAWNSHOPKIM'SMARKETCALLHOMECHEAPPHONECARDS!

A block from my apartment building, I stopped at the 7-Eleven to waste the few minutes my shortcut across the bridge had saved. I spent five minutes debating the merits of blue raspberry versus cherry limeade Slurpee, before blending them into a disgusting purple slush. Geena was strolling around the store like she owned it and was taking inventory, and when she finally made it to the Slurpee machine, she picked grape and was quick about it. We waited in line at the same time, but not together. The man behind the counter grinned as I laid my change on the counter with one hand and tried to balance my Slurpee and balloon in the other. He pointed upward at the bobbing surface, and read: Congratulations. He smiled and looked me over.

"You had a baby?"

I rolled my eyes and shook my head.

"Someone in your family had a baby?"

I stared at him stupidly. His face looked open, like he was waiting for an answer so he knew the right expression to make. I wanted to hit him or I wanted to say something clever or I wanted to leave, with or without my stupid Slurpee. I was waiting to be a different person when Geena stepped around from behind me. I thought for a minute she was getting in my face to laugh at me, but she grabbed my arm, hard, making little indentations for each of her violet fingernails, and dragged me toward the door, calling over her shoulder, "Nah, mister, she ain't pregnant, at our school they give you a balloon for giving all the teachers blow jobs. It don't really mean shit."

Outside, I walked faster and hoped his English wasn't good enough that he knew what *blow job* meant. Geena laughed.

"You didn't pay for that," I said, pointing at her Slurpee.

"No," she said. "Didn't pay for the cigarettes, either."

I waited for shouts or sirens but none came, so I followed her lead, matching her stride and imagining my steps clicked like hers. Our bravado peeled a little as we crossed the parking lot and avoided looking up at the men who hung out in front of the store all day, looking for work, or drinking, or both. It was after three, so the hope of day work had mostly faded and the drinking was in full swing. They grunted appreciatively at the bodies we hadn't quite figured out what to do with yet, and we shrank into ourselves at their cat-calls, as if blushing would make our breasts and behinds less promi-nent. On the next block we were cool again, walked tall and touched mailboxes and fence posts and other things that weren't ours. Geena lit a cigarette and I watched her smoke.

"Thank you," I said to Geena, once we'd reached my building. I hoped she wouldn't make me explain what I was thanking her for.

"Don't be embarrassed 'cause other people are dumb," said Geena.

Geena Johnson was my friend. Maybe not right away, but things could happen quick like that back then. Geena came by the day after the Slurpee incident. Geena taught me how to dance and how to steal. Geena dragged me to cheerleading tryouts and threw her arms around me when we both made the JV squad. Geena also told me I'd have to do her homework sometimes so she wouldn't get put on academic probation. Old Crystal would have had something to say about this, but I was suddenly a girl with lip liner and red and blue pom-poms. I'd just nodded.

Out of respect for Geena, or maybe it was fear, nobody from Eastdale really messed with me, but nobody talked to me, either. They looked at me curiously, the way they might have looked at a one-eyed kitten or baby bird Geena had picked up one day and begun to carry everywhere. I carried books everywhere and, without really meaning to, ignored everyone but Geena. On the bus to away games I sat in the back reading while the rest of the squad acted like girls were supposed to: Geena traded raunchy insults with the football players, Violeta and April gave each other makeovers, Tien stared into space, and Jesse perched seductively on somebody's lap until one of the coaches made her get up and saunter poutily to her own seat.

Football season was almost over by the first time I made myself noticed. Things had been louder than usual, and I stopped reading *The Souls of Black Folk* for long enough to hear what everyone was complaining about. We were on our way to our second-to-last game of the season—one we were probably going to lose—but all anyone could talk about was next week's rivalry game. The county had structured the football league so that every school had a major rival and the season ended with games between rivals, which were played for a prize. Our rival school was Stonewall Jackson, a new school in the middle of the new gated community of Hillcrest, the place where people in Lakewood kept threatening to move. Its newness made the whole concept of Rivalry Week stupid. There hadn't been time for any history of rivalry between Lee and Jackson High Schools, and there wouldn't have been any rivalry in the present if the school board hadn't set it up that way. Next week's varsity game was known as the Rebel Yell. The winner got to display an old sword that was said to be a Confederate relic, though its exact circumstances were unknown and any history we were given for it usually turned out to be invented.

• • •

"I can't believe that lady," Jason Simmons called from a few seats ahead of us. "Like she don't know that's the whole fucking point of Rivalry Week."

"Whatever," Eric Manns called back. "I don't give a fuck what Mrs. Peterson says, eggs and toilet paper is some bitch-ass white-boy shit, anyway. You would not catch me up in Hillcrest trying to out-run the popo over a damn football game."

Jason shook his head. Mrs. Peterson, Lee's head guidance counselor, had made an announcement about Rivalry Week during morning assembly. Traditionally, the week before the end-of-season games was marked by a chain of vandalisms, but apparently the school board was exasperated by the annual cleanup efforts. *If any act of vandalism is traced to a high school in this county,* Mrs. Peterson had declared, *the cost of cleanup will be taken out of that school's activity budget.*

I hadn't been paying attention at the time and assumed that the chorus of boos was just a general reaction to Mrs. Peterson's voice. The woman was thoroughly disliked; hatred of her was one of the few things upon which everyone at Robert E. Lee High School agreed. The Eastdale kids hated her because she had a habit of hanging up on people's parents when they didn't speak English instead of getting a translator, as was county policy, and she was known for suspending people based on their zip codes rather than their behavior. At a school assembly last year, she'd blamed the dropping standardized test scores on immigrant kids who, before arriving in Eastdale, had been "living in jungles."

I hated her because she'd tried to talk me out of honors classes and only signed off on my schedule because I'd threatened to go to the principal. I was an accident; I'd slipped through our school's de facto segregation and she wasn't happy about it. I had been dealing with people like her since the third grade, when I'd been shipped off to a "gifted" school as a reward for outsmarting standardized tests. The magnet elementary and middle schools were the Lake County School District's last line of defense against the evaporation of its upwardly mobile white people. The Lakewood PTA had tried to get a new magnet high school built, smack in the middle of Lakewood, and, when that failed, tried to have Eastdale students rezoned to a high school five miles farther away, but the county comptroller wasn't having it. They settled for an honors wing, which housed everyone whose standardized test scores placed them into honors classes, or everyone whose parents knew that you could pay a private psychologist to declare your child a genius even if the school's official test thought otherwise. Essentially, the honors wing housed all of Lakewood, and me.

I wasn't sure why my Lakewood classmates hated Mrs. Peterson. She seemed to view herself as their principal guardian and defender, but they called her "the evil chipmunk" and did bucktoothed impersonations of her behind her back. She did have buckteeth, along with a dumpy figure and a wardrobe of seasonally themed sweatshirts. Sometimes I almost felt sorry for her, the way kids laughed.

"What the fuck are they going to take out of our budget, anyway?" Jason went on. "We ain't got shit to begin with."

That was true: much to the chagrin of our Lakewood classmates,

we'd had the lowest budget in the county for years. Jason's real problem was that Rivalry Week was usually a rite of passage from JV
to varsity. By the look on his face I could tell Jason was comparing
the Hillcrest Police Department to whatever alternative initiation
scheme the varsity players would come up with, and thinking he'd
rather take his chances with the cops.

"Look, I ain't even worried about the game," Eric announced.
"Fuck the game, fuck Rivalry Week, I ain't worried about anything
but the fine-ass girl I'm taking to the party afterward."

"Nigga, who the fuck wants to go with you?"

Eric surveyed the back of the bus as if looking for a comeback.

"Antisocial back there might be all right if she'd put that book
down for a second."

I looked up. It was the first time all season I'd been addressed
directly and I wasn't prepared with a clever retort.

"Aww, leave her alone. She probably got homework," Jason
called.

"That book ain't homework."

"How the fuck you know what homework they got in honors
English? You barely know what homework you got in plain old regular English."

"Negro, I go to Robert E. Lee High School, I know damn well
ain't no *Souls of Black Folk* required reading. Maybe *Black Folk
Ain't Got No Souls, Who the Hell Told 'Em to Stop Picking Cotton,
Anyway?*"

The people around us laughed; hearing that he had an audience,
Eric lifted himself onto his knees and kept going.

"Don't know why the fuck you laughing, Garcia. The next book they read is *Mexicans Ain't Got No Souls, Either, and Them Mothafuckas Don't Even Speak English*."

He turned back to me. "Or do I got it all wrong, Antisocial? Go 'head, drop some knowledge on me."

I stared back and started to open my mouth, but Geena was quicker.

"Look, she's reading 'cause you idiots ain't worth her time. Now sit the fuck down before I beat your black ass and then call your mama so she can do it again."

"Ooh," said Eric, throwing up his hands in an exaggerated gesture of defeat. "I don't want Geena to beat my ass and call my mama."

He sat down, though, and I had a sudden sense of the next four years passing something like this.

"I know what to do about the new vandalism policy."

Even Geena whirled her head around in shock. The whole back of the bus looked at me expectantly. I could feel my heart racing and wondered when it had started mattering what they thought of me.

"Later," I said, nodding toward the coaches. "After the varsity game, so the varsity team can hear too."

Geena hardly spoke to me all afternoon. If I fucked this up I was on my own, that much was clear. Geena had helped me out, but she wasn't about to go down with me.

We met outside school after the varsity game. The varsity players had in fact waited around to see what I had to say. I took deep breaths and played with the zipper on my cheerleading jacket, feeling something like the leader of an underground crime syndicate. My jacket said ROBERT E. LEE CHEERLEADING on the back, but it was the front that I stared down at: *Crystal 2000. Crystal, 2000. Crystal 2000!* I liked to think of it that way, like a brand-new kind of Crystal: *Crystal 2000! Cheerleading Goddess, Criminal Extraordinaire.* While I was mentally branding myself, Tyrone Holmes, the senior quarterback, interrupted and prompted me to speak.

"So, umm, I was thinking, like . . ."

I could hear the varsity cheerleaders giggling at my speech and began again, flexing my newly credible Eastdale voice.

"I mean, I'm saying, though, we fuck with Stonewall, we get in trouble. First there's the cops, and then there's the school board, and we don't need all that. But if they fuck with us, it's them that gets in trouble."

"You think they're dumb enough to do that?"

"They don't have to be." I shook my head. "If we do the school but we use their colors and make it look like it was them, they get fined and we get the money."

"You think we should fuck up our own school?" Jason asked.

"Why not?" I asked. "Anybody care about this place?"

Tyrone nodded and grinned at me. "You know, Antisocial, you might be all right."

"Told you," said Geena.

A week later, we met in the parking lot of Walgreens, supplies in hand. A few seniors with old, beat-up cars carted about twenty of us to the parking lot in the middle of the night, where we split up to carry out our duties. Tyrone and Eric spray-painted the main entrance blue and silver—Stonewall Jackson's colors—while their teammates

Rafael and Delos broke a few of the back windows. ("Don't do the downstairs classrooms: the heat doesn't work right and it will get too cold," Geena reminded them.) Some of the JV players TP'd the fence, while most of the cheerleaders chalked the track and the main sidewalk. We were not especially creative. *Fuck* was the worst word most of us could think of: *Fuck Robert E. Lee*, *Fuck you broke Gooks, Spics and Niggers*, *Fuck this Ghetto Ass School, Stonewall Rules, Go Generals!* Geena and I had the honor of vandalizing the school statue. We dumped a bucket of blue paint over Robert E. Lee's head and painted long, thick stripes of silver paint over the plaque at the bottom. A final *Go Stonewall!* spray-painted on the outside fence, while Tien stood sentry and watched for passing cars, would be enough to get us off the hook completely.

Afterward we were not so careful. A bunch of us piled into Rafael's van and drove screaming and swerving up and down Leesburg Pike. We smelled strongly of paint fumes and opened all the windows in order to stick our heads out and gulp down fresh air. It was November, but there were too many of us in the van to be cold, we were packed in tight and squeezed against each other. I could vaguely feel Tyrone's hand creeping up my thigh, but the dizzying combination of paint fumes and the wine cooler Geena had given me earlier kept me from being sure I should do something about it. Rafael swerved into Lakewood and we drove up their hills, tearing past their mammoth brick houses, circling the private beaches built around their man-made lake, where small groups of our classmates gathered for parties on weekends. Eric rode shotgun and blasted the radio while Geena and I screamed out the windows, and the cold air and the hot van and the beat—because there was always a beat—became their own universe. It was shattered by the screech of sirens in the distance, and it was over that quickly. Rafael made a sharp left and took the back roads into Eastdale, but not before Geena stuck her head out of the window a final time and screamed to the empty echo behind us, "Fuck you, too, fucking cops!" and then collapsed giggling in my lap. We had driven all through Lakewood, but when I got back to my apartment and sleepily collapsed on the living room sofa that doubled as my bed, I was not a bit jealous, not at all. They had houses, they had money, they damn near ran the school, but they still had nothing that was half as exciting as Geena.

We lost the football game. A couple of the Lakewood kids seemed sad about this: they'd genuinely wanted that sword. "Probably to cut our heads off with," Jason said. On our part, the loss was overshadowed by the enthusiastic response to the news that Stonewall Jackson was going to have to reschedule their prom. We knew they'd get the money back, but it was a victory nonetheless. The school held an assembly to address the vandalism. The senior class adviser chided Jackson for "not only committing such a childish act but refusing to take responsibility for it even after the fact." The Jackson football team had claimed over and over again that they'd had nothing to do with it, that we'd probably done it ourselves to get them in trouble. Apparently it didn't occur to anyone to believe them. In the school board's mind, we still had loyalties. Mrs. Peterson gave a long speech about embracing diversity—rather like a wolf giving a speech on embracing sheep—and said it was mystifying that anyone would even make such a charge against us. Geena and I sat straight-faced and said nothing. It had been our experience that white people were very easily mystified.

After that, my nickname went from Antisocial to CeeCee, and Geena and I got permanent seats at the Eastdale senior lunch table. My classmates in honors weren't sure what to make of my sudden transformation. After being harassed for most of elementary school, I'd realized that the more invisible I was, the more likely it was they'd reserve their cruelty for each other. In middle school, I'd been the girl sitting quietly in the back of the class, taking copious notes and wearing shapeless sweaters. It worked. They'd all started hating each other instead of me. For the first time in my life, I was the only person who never cried in the bathroom during lunchtime. My new high visibility violated the unspoken terms of our *détente*. I was suddenly a girl who wore stilettos and hip-huggers, who ran into class just before the bell rang, shouting good-byes all the way down to the end of the hallway. I was *still* a girl who knew more right answers than they did, which was the real source of the trouble—I'd gone from being an anomaly to being an impossibility.

Walking out of World History one afternoon, I heard Caitlyn Murphy say loudly, "How in the hell can she walk in those jeans?"

"How in the hell can she walk with that ass, more like," Libby Carlisle joined in.

"Well," said Anna James, "I'm glad she's turning into a crack whore. Now I don't have to worry about her messing up my class rank."

I told Geena about this conversation after lunch, then thought no more of it until I went looking for her after school. Vi finally told me she was cornering Libby and Anna in the parking lot. To this day, I don't know the exact terms of that confrontation: Geena wasn't talking and it was a full year before Libby and Anna got up the nerve to even look at me again, let alone speak to me. Whatever the case, Geena got suspended for two days and no one fucked with me after that. I perfected the art of smiling cruelly, then ran out of school to Geena, and the football field, and the city late at night, to everything that was bright and noisy and newly beautiful.

We were not always laughing. When Geena's mom was hospitalized with a tumor that turned out to be benign, I cut school for three days to hold Geena's hand in the hospital waiting room. Later, when the attendance woman said the unexcused absences meant we would both automatically fail for the semester, I got a sympathetic young ER resident to write doctor's notes for both of us. When my dad lost his job and I couldn't stand to be in the house and hear my parents budgeting money in terse voices, Geena invented reasons why I had to sleep over at her place every night. When Geena had her abortion, I went with her and covered for her with everyone who wanted to know why she wasn't laughing like usual. When I swallowed a bottle of Tylenol for no real reason I could think of, Geena stuck her fingers down my throat until I vomited, and through my vomit and her tears screamed until I promised never to do it again. These were the things we never talked about, but they were our things nonetheless.

• • •

In the spring of my junior year, Mrs. Peterson sent an office aid to pull me out of class right before lunch. A chorus of *oohs* greeted the announcement that Mrs. Peterson wanted to see me. In the waiting area, I smiled weakly at Mrs. Sanchez, the receptionist, hoping she might give me a heads-up on what I was here for. She only smiled back at me. Inside her office, Mrs. Peterson grinned at me with her big chipmunk teeth. I had never been so scared to be smiled at.

"Crystal," she started, and I fought the urge to tell her that was not my name anymore and hadn't been for quite some time.

"We're very proud of the work you've done since coming to Robert E. Lee. Your record here has been truly impressive."

I was afraid she was going to expel me. I thought of the worst things I'd done in recent history and prepared myself to explain to her why going to Taco Bell during lunch, hooking up with Jason in his basement, and loaning my fake ID to a freshman cheerleader were not offenses for which she could legitimately kick me out of school.

"Every year," she continued, "we send one student to the state summer academy. I am pleased to tell you that this year you are our nominee."

I was so shocked that my reflexive thank-you got caught in my throat. She babbled on about the state summer academy and how good it would look on my college applications. I sat back catching bits and pieces. The seminar was on government and philosophy, which meant I'd get to read more of the stuff everyone thought I was a freak for actually enjoying, but if it had been a seminar on decorating kitchens, I still would have said yes. Being nominated by the school meant that I'd get free room and board at the university where the program was held. I was thinking it was amazing that anyone would pay for me to get away from my life for a few weeks. I was thinking also that I was not stupid. I read the papers: I knew the governor had just started a state commission on the achievement gap between white and minority students. I could picture Mrs. Peterson pouring the state investigator a cup of tea and shrugging and saying, "*Crystal* has done beautifully, and has been rewarded for it. If her friends showed the same motivation . . ."

Mrs. Peterson was still talking in the present. I snapped back into the conversation when I heard Geena's name, followed by:

"—nearly on academic probation again. I hope you take note of this. Be careful about the company you keep."

I wondered what kind of company she kept. I opened my mouth to defend Geena, but knew that right then I couldn't afford to make Mrs. Peterson angry. Besides, what was keeping Geena off academic probation was me doing her homework, and Mrs. Peterson didn't need to know that. I shut my mouth and left her office.

I knew Geena would be mad; I just didn't know how mad, or how soon. After school she asked me why I had missed lunch, and I told her I'd been in Mrs. Peterson's office for our lunch period and she'd given me a pass to eat during B lunch instead.

"What the fuck did she want?" Geena asked.

I swallowed. Geena and I were supposed to work at the Baskin-Robbins again this summer in order to save money for a week of cheerleading camp and an end-of-the-summer beach trip that we planned to take together. I told her all at once, letting the words tumble together and repeating over and over again that the program was free.

She was quiet for a minute after I finished.

"So, Mrs. Peterson is, like, your friend now?"

"Not my friend. I mean, I'm sure she's just doing it because it looks good, and besides, I have the best grades. If she didn't pick me, she'd have had to explain why. But whatever, you know? It's not like she really likes me."

"Yeah, OK."

Geena started walking down the hallway and I followed her.

"Geena, what do you want me to do?" I called. I didn't mean for it to come out like a question, but it did, anyway.

She kept walking. I walked home alone, and I took the long way.

I let the promise of summer comfort me while Geena avoided me. Violeta and April became Geena's new best girlfriends. I was somewhat consoled by the fact that it took two people to replace me. Vi made a point of telling everyone that she'd gone to middle school with me and I'd been a bougie bitch then too. I started to eat lunch in the library again. If Geena thought she could make me lonely enough to change my mind about summer school, she'd vastly underestimated my capacity for loneliness. I'd perfected lonely in the third grade.

The summer passed quickly. I spent most of my time in my dorm room reading. It was quieter than my life had ever been and I didn't mind it. Geena and her anger were a million miles away from the college campus. I thought occasionally of the parties I was missing, of varsity practice and what I'd do with all my free time when I wasn't on the squad next fall. Geena wouldn't be on the squad, either: without me to do her homework, she'd failed two classes and wasn't eligible to cheer. Mostly I didn't think of high school at all. I read Plato and Aristotle and the Constitution, and in those moments I felt tremendously insignificant.

I walked around alone often, but my roommate for the summer didn't find my quietness strange at all. Occasionally we'd look up from reading and smile shyly. I'd always thought the whole world was just a bigger version of Lee High School—a line running down the middle of it and people on either side telling me that I didn't really belong there. There were still people like that at the summer academy, but I also met a handful of people who seemed to understand me on my own terms. A girl with a long black ponytail offered to be my roommate if we both got into the university. I thanked her, but in my mind I thought I'd like to go much, much farther away.

By the time school started again, I had almost forgotten what I was missing. I wasn't lonely anymore; I was just alone. That was the luxury I had then: Geena had already made me possible. Her boldness, which I'd always thought I'd been borrowing from her, had become mine in ways I didn't realize until she was gone. I didn't flinch around people who didn't like me; I didn't feel anymore like being myself was something for which I owed the world an apology.

Then again, if you believed the rumors, everyone was past the point of apology: they were busy trying to find a way to impose themselves on the world. I heard that Eric had replaced the engine in his car and gotten it to go 140 down the Pike, but it sounded like empty boasting; and as much as Vi was enjoying her rise in status, I had trouble believing that she'd actually make the freshmen cheerleaders carve player's names into their thighs with a penknife. It was senior year, and the world as I knew it was undoing itself. The more adult everyone got on paper, the dumber they got in real life. Libby Carlisle celebrated her early admission to Stanford by nearly OD'ing on coke; the senior class president got drunk one night and crashed his car into the side of a church.

We were not so much tempting fate as bargaining with it. With the sincere fatalism only teenagers can manage, we assumed that what happened before the year was out would determine what our lives would be forever after, and no one seemed thrilled about their prospects. Life became an insistent preoccupation with what happened next. The military recruitment office was full of people I'd known since elementary school and never pegged as particularly violent or patriotic. They weren't, most of them, but the general attitude was that the military beat working at McDonald's—at least you got to go somewhere. I started noticing how very few people actually went anywhere; the parties I used to go to with Geena had always been frequented by people who had graduated years earlier but were still around, working, or at Bailey, the local community college. Seniors started to amuse themselves by noting how fat people had gotten or how many kids they had or what kind of piece of junk they were driving; they knew it was their last chance to feel superior to anybody.

The New Year came and went; I drank sparkling apple cider with my parents and watched the ball drop on television. It was the end of January before Geena spoke to me again. She appeared at my locker after school, shifting nervously, which was strange, because I hardly ever saw Geena look nervous.

"Look," she said, "this is bullshit. You wanna go to the mall after school?"

I neglected to point out that the bullshit was mostly her doing. I nodded, grabbed my purse out of my locker, and followed her to the beat-up old blue Tercel she'd bought with the money she'd saved that summer, the money we hadn't used for our beach trip. It was as if the light came on and I suddenly noticed it had been dark for months.

As quickly as they'd forgotten me, the crowd took me back. Geena let me know who'd been talking the most shit about me and we made a point of ostracizing them. We made up for lost time with a few long talks and a lot of off-campus lunches. We never exactly talked about the fight, and if anyone was rude enough to bring it up, they met both of our icy stares and shut up quickly.

By the end of March, I was on edge, waiting to find out where I'd gotten into college and whether I'd have the money to go. Geena was in danger of not graduating, but didn't seem particularly concerned about it. AP exams were over and the final grades that would be used for class ranking were out. The teachers knew they couldn't really keep us in school. I spent a lot of time driving around with Geena in the middle of the day. Some sophomore girls claimed a section of our lunch table and we didn't even bother putting them in their place. We could already feel our world slipping away from us.

I think it was them that finally got to Geena, them and the four fat college acceptance letters I got in April. Walking past the senior lockers one day, we saw one of the new girls making out with her senior boyfriend. Geena shook her head and rolled her eyes in my direction, like *At least we don't have to fuck people to be popular.* I nodded back, and mouthed, *Amateurs.*

Geena came up with the prank idea after that. She showed up at my locker after school with a sour apple lollipop in her mouth.

"Hey," she started, "we should do something. Like a senior prank."

"Geena. White kids do senior pranks. When we try it, they're called felonies."

"I thought you were practically one of them, anyway."

I shot Geena a warning look and she dropped the subject. Still, I could see her getting more and more upset by the little things. She made a point of making Sophomore Slut Girl change lunch tables one day, coming *this close* to physically removing her. She talked with increasing frequency about the fact that she wasn't getting a diploma. She was of two minds on the matter. One moment she'd shrug and say, "What the fuck do I want a stupid piece of paper for anyway?" The next, she'd shake her head and say, "They ought to at least give me something. Much time as I spent in this dumb-ass school."

I got used to her mood swings and went along with them. It was easier than arguing, and I didn't object much anyway. When Libby

Carlisle got named prom queen, Geena launched into a ten-minute tirade on how she was the ugliest, bitchiest, dishwater-blondest excuse for a prom queen she'd ever heard of.

"Don't worry about Libby Carlisle," I said. "Libby Carlisle is about to encounter the unpleasant reality that the world does not revolve around her ass, and when she finally accepts that reality she'll need Valium and an exotic lover to get through her boring and frustrated life."

Geena laughed. "That's why I love you, CeeCee. You're so full of shit."

Geena stopped coming to school altogether. She wasn't going to graduate anyway, so there wasn't much point. I went to the obligatory senior class events and showed up for the final exams that teachers administered halfheartedly. The rest of my time was spent camped out on Geena's living room floor, watching bad talk shows and soap operas. Geena was getting animated again by the prospect of end-of-year parties. Prom was too expensive, but April was having a semiformal in her backyard the same night, and we were excited enough about it. Geena and I went dress shopping at what everyone called the Ghetto Mall, though you knew by who was talking whether or not they meant it affectionately. I liked the dress shop, its awning unpretentiously proclaiming DRESSES, its owner a chatty Vietnamese woman who was good at eyeballing women and knowing what size they needed, even if they argued with her about it. I spent an hour eyeing the intricate beadwork of the Quinceañera dresses, lined up in the window like cakes with brightly colored icing, before settling on something slinky and black. The day of the party, Geena curled my hair and put red lipstick on me, sashaying around the room in her own deep-purple strapless sheath.

"Damn, CeeCee. Remember what a geek you were when I found you?"

"I'm not a puppy." I pouted. "You didn't find me. And anyway, I'm still a geek. So there."

I stuck my tongue out and fell back on her bed.

"Well, you're a hundred percent better than you were," she snapped back, curling her eyelashes in the cracked full-length mirror on her wall. "And sit the hell up before you smash the curls I just put in your head."

I don't know what we were expecting the party to be like, but it was just like every other party we'd been to since freshman year, except nobody was wearing jeans. The music echoed all the way down the block and the lawn smelled like a weak mixture of beer, weed, and vomit. The smell and the heat clung to everyone there, but all we could hear was laughter. On the back porch lay a pile of abandoned heels, shawls, jackets and ties: girls had realized how uncomfortable it was to be beautiful, and the few boys who'd bothered to take the semiformal status of the party seriously had found themselves outnumbered and done a quick ruffling of their appearances.

On the front lawn, Vi was trying to teach two freshmen how to dance cumbia, the beat from Jay-Z blaring inside the house throwing off the rhythm she was counting out. Inside, people danced on beat, some pressed so close together it was hard to tell one body from another. Others skipped the dancing all together; all of the bedroom doors were locked and April was more than happy to tell us who was in each of them. She was also slightly tipsy, and melodramatically complained about the red stain spreading across her living room carpet: someone had spilled a punch bowl full of Alizé. It smelled sickly-sweet and looked like blood.

Geena and I ended up in the garage. We could only stand around and look superior for so long before we just looked stupid.

"So," said Geena, taking a sip of her wine cooler, "you going to graduation tomorrow?"

"I have to go," I said, taking a bigger swallow of mine than I intended. Stray drops of pink liquid trickled down the front of my dress.

"Right." Geena nodded. "I ain't going. They're just gonna gimme a fake piece of paper that says I didn't graduate and would I like information about some damn GED programs."

I swallowed again. "I have to go," I repeated. "I'm the valedictorian."

Geena laughed. "Like you haven't been waiting your whole life for this shit."

"I've been killing myself my whole life for this shit. They don't have to expect me to be all happy about it."

"Oh, right," said Geena, smirking. "Poor you."

"I didn't mean it like that."

"You always mean it like that."

"Look," I said. "I don't even wanna go tomorrow. I have to. That's all. No one will listen anyway. Half the parents don't care at all about any part of graduation except when their kid's name gets called. And the half of the ones that do care are going to be so pissed it's me speaking and not their *gifted* child that they'll spend the whole speech bitching. The only two people listening will be my parents, which means I can't say anything I actually want to say, which is fuck you all very much for making me miserable since the third grade, I'm out."

"If it were me, I'd say that."

"Yeah, well. I can't. Anyway, Mrs. Peterson already approved my real speech. It's about success and obstacles and respect and bullshit."

"Well," said Geena, "I guess Mrs. Peterson's opinion counts more than anyone else's."

I started to laugh, but she wasn't kidding.

"You really don't want to do this, I can get you out of it," Geena said. "We can tell every-damn-body how you really feel. You and me."

It was enough that I didn't say no. Geena picked her shoes up off the garage floor where she'd kicked them aside and was already on her way out the door.

"You coming?" she called, dangling her car keys.

With a halfhearted last look at Tien throwing up on April's front lawn, I followed Geena to her car. A few minutes later we were parked in front of her cousin Ray's house a few blocks away. He ran a kind of automotive/construction business, in that there were usually broken-down cars parked on the front lawn, and occasionally he fixed something, and occasionally someone actually paid him for it. I didn't ask what we were doing there. The lights were off, but Geena had a house key, and for a few minutes she walked back and forth between the car and the garage, putting things in the trunk: paint, a toolbox, a six-pack she'd stolen from the garage refrigerator.

"You aiight, CeeCee?" she asked when she got back in the car.

"Yeah, I'm good." I stared out of the window and tried to look disinterested.

"You want to go home, I'll take you home."

"I'm not going home," I said.

Geena didn't respond, and I stayed quiet. The roads were all familiar. Within minutes I was looking at my high school in the dark. Geena pulled over in the back parking lot, right beside the football field. The field had been done over for graduation. A wooden stage had been erected in the middle of it, red, white, and blue circular banners were draped across the bottoms of the stage and the bleachers. A gold banner, stretched between two posts beside the stage, read: CONGRATULATIONS, ROBERT E. LEE CLASS OF 2000. In front of the stage, rows and rows of white plastic chairs had been set up for the senior class.

Geena got the six-pack out of the trunk and we sat in the car for a while, drinking and talking. I didn't even like beer, but it gave me something to do besides look at Geena, who seemed sadder than I'd ever seen her, or the football field, all done up and ready for me to be a person I had never wanted to be.

"Remember freshman year?" Geena asked.

"Yeah."

"It was like we ran things."

"We didn't, though. It just felt that way because we were kids."

She made circles on the dashboard with her pointer finger. "I'm going to miss you."

"I'm not going that far. It's a three-hour train ride," I answered, deliberately avoiding the reality that our lives were to be measured in a different kind of distance.

"So, you really don't want to do this tomorrow?" Geena asked.

"No," I said quickly.

"Bet you they won't have a ceremony if the stage is all fucked up," said Geena.

We got out of the car and I followed Geena to the stage, carrying the things she'd gotten from Ray's. When we got to the field, Geena put down what she was carrying and walked the rest of the way to the stage. She climbed the stairs and walked around for a minute, pausing for a moment behind the podium. She spoke as if speaking into a microphone, but there was no mic, and from the other end of the field, I couldn't hear a word she said. When she was done, she hopped off the stage, forgoing the stairs, and handed me a can of spray paint.

"You serious about this?" she asked.

By way of answering, I uncapped the can and pointed it at her for a second, grinning. Then I walked to the far end of the football field, by the opposing team's goalposts. I wanted to say the one thing that would make everybody see themselves for what they really were, but I had no special insight into the human condition. I had only one thing to say, the thing I'd been swallowing every day since I had first been confronted with the entitled faces of my "gifted" Lakewood classmates, since I'd first heard the taunts of the Eastdale neighborhood kids, who would have ignored me my whole life if it hadn't been for Geena, who would have never understood that I was angry on their behalf as much as on mine. YOU ARE NOT AS SPECIAL AS YOU THINK YOU ARE, I sprayed in huge letters on the grass. I shook the paint can when I'd finished, but it was empty.

"Geena," I called, "I'm not done. Bring me another paint can."

But she didn't answer me, and when I turned around, she wasn't doing anything herself, just leaning against the stage, smoking a Newport and looking at me with some mix of concern and confusion. She walked over to where I was standing.

"Come on," she said, dropping her cigarette and taking my hand. "Let's go. I shouldn't have talked you into this."

"No," I said, "I'm not finished. And you didn't talk me into it."

I wanted to sign my name—my real one. I wanted, for the first time in my life, the world to see my real self, my whole one. I walked over to where Geena had left the paint cans and went back to my work of art. FUCK YOU, I wrote. LOVE, CRYSTAL.

"Crystal," Geena yelled when I was halfway done, "are you drunk or are you stupid? You can't put your real goddamn name! Put mine!"

But I wasn't drunk or stupid, just tipsy and angry, and it wasn't about Geena anymore, or even about tomorrow. I saw Geena coming over with a small brush and paint can in her hand, watched her dump it over the *C* in my name. I expected it to be swallowed up in fresh paint, but it remained clear, like Geena had just splashed it with water, and something sharp hit my nostrils.

"Shit!" Geena shrieked. "That was paint thinner. Fucking Ray."

For a second we started to laugh together at Ray's ineptitude, but then I saw the faintest shimmer of orange a few feet from where she'd spilled it, remembered the cigarette she'd dropped earlier. I grabbed her hand and we raced breathlessly down to the other end of the field. I was still thinking it wasn't a big deal, that we could grab the water hose attached to the back of the school and put it out before it got any bigger, but by the time we turned around, the fire had scorched the whole spot where the letter C had been, and was starting to spread from there. It was almost summer, and the grass on the football field was dry and brown. I had heard once that our football field was a Civil War graveyard; watching the fire slither outward from one blade of glass to the next, I believed it. The fire was still small in area and low to the ground, but if nothing stopped it, it would reach the wooden stage, and then perhaps the wooden bleachers, and eventually the trees behind them, then finally the houses behind it. I looked at the fifty-yard line, where the grass no longer said CRYSTAL, and above it, where it still said YOU ARE NOT AS SPECIAL AS YOU THINK YOU ARE but wouldn't for long. I ran for the pay phone in the school's front parking lot, Geena behind me. I had just picked up the phone when Geena reached past me and pressed down the receiver, her nails glittering purple against the metal.

"Go," she said, her face so close to mine I could see my eyes reflected in hers. Her mascara had pooled into black smudges under her eyes; I knew I couldn't look much better. "This isn't little-kid shit anymore. They're gonna find out who called. They're gonna look."

I understood her but I didn't move at first, not until I imagined myself answering questions at a police station, the look on my parents' faces when they got the phone call, the look on Libby Carlisle's face when she got to give my speech tomorrow, when she got to tell everyone she'd been right about me all along. I started to back away slowly.

"You wanna let the fucking school burn down, stay," said Geena. She wouldn't take her hand off of the receiver.

I stared at Geena for a long second. Then I took off running, stopping in the middle of the parking lot to take off my heels. I kept running, the asphalt stinging my feet through my panty hose. Halfway up the hill behind the school, I stopped to look back, vaguely recalling Sunday school and Lot's wife turning into a pillar of salt. Already I could hear sirens in the distance. I watched Geena sitting on the curb beside the pay phone, fists curled backward into cushions for her chin. She looked small and still and ready. I turned then, shut my eyes, and ran breathlessly toward the dam. I didn't stop again until I had crossed the bridge and hopped the fence that took me back to Eastdale. On the other side, I stopped to catch my breath, and then kept running, knowing even then that a better person would have turned around.

ACKNOWLEDGMENTS

Throughout the writing process I've had the support of my immediate and extended family and stepfamilies, who have lent me their homes, their money, and occasionally the details of their lives, which are better than any I could invent. There are too many people and favors for me to list all of them, but consider me eternally grateful. Many thanks to my mother, who taught me to be honest; my grandmother, who taught me the value of a good story; and my father, who taught me how much you can say without words.

This book would not have been possible had I not been so lucky in my friends, who let me show up on their doorsteps and sleep on their sofas, helped me move back and forth across the country, made me feel at home in new cities, answered their phones in the middle of the night, and told me when to hang up and get back to work. Among them: Jeanne Elone, Miriam Aguila, Dana Renee Thompson, Lailan Huen,

Acknowledgments

Teresa Hernandez, Ileana Mendez-Peñate, Reina Gossett, Nell Geiser, Rachel McPherson, Laleh Khadivi, Sean Hill, April Wilder, Jennifer Key, Joel Creswell, Elizabeth Snipes, Sarah Wiggin, and Tiara Izquierdo. Thank you. Special thanks to Alexis Pauline Gumbs, for so often being my first and favorite reader. I am thankful for the support, financial and otherwise, that I've received from numerous institutions. The Iowa Writers' Workshop gave me time, money, and, most important, faith that my writing mattered to an audience—all rare and valuable for emerging writers. Special thanks to Connie Brothers, Jim McPherson, and Adam Haslett. The Wisconsin Institute for Creative Writing is one of the best places a writer could ever call home. I'm grateful to the entire UW–Madison creative writing faculty, and the late Carol Houck Smith, for making my fellowship year possible. Special thanks to Jesse Lee Kercheval for being a constant source of sound advice. Thank you to Columbia University, especially the Kluge and Mellon scholars programs, for giving me the room to try these stories in their earliest forms and to Missouri State University and American University, for giving me homes while I finished them.

I'm indebted to my amazing agent, Ayesha Pande, who is a fantastic supporter and advocate and fielder of frantic phone calls and emails; my editor, Sarah McGrath, who gave the book so much of her time, energy, and attention; and her editorial assistant, Sarah Stein. Thank you to all the editors and journals who have published stories I've written, and to those who took the time to send encouraging or instructive rejections. Special thanks to *Phoebe*, which took a chance on my first short story, and *The Paris Review*, which has been so supportive of my work. Many, many thanks to Radhika Jones for her work on the story *Virgins*.